BY JOHN FANTE
AVAILABLE FROM ECCO

The Saga of Arturo Bandini:
Wait Until Spring, Bandini
The Road to Los Angeles
Ask the Dust
Dreams from Bunker Hill

Full of Life
The Brotherhood of the Grape
The Wine of Youth: Selected Stories of John Fante
1933 Was a Bad Year
West of Rome
The Big Hunger: Stories 1932–1959
Selected Letters 1932–1981
The John Fante Reader

John Fante

Wait Until Spring, Bandini

ecco

An Imprint of HarperCollinsPublishers

HarperCollins books may be purchased for educational, business, or sales promotional use. For information, please e-mail the Special Markets Department at SPsales@harpercollins.com.

First Ecco edition 2002
Previously published by Black Sparrow Press

The Library of Congress has catalogued a previous edition as follows:

Fante, John, 1909-1983
    Wait until spring, Bandini.

    Reprint. Originally published: New York : Stackpole, 1938.
    I. Title.
PS3511.A594W3   1983   813'.5'2   82-24412
ISBN 0-87685-555-9
ISBN 0-87685-554-0 (pbk.)

$PrintCode

This book is dedicated to my mother,
Mary Fante, with love and devotion;
and to my father, Nick Fante, with
love and admiration.

Preface

Now that I am an old man I cannot look back upon *Wait Until Spring, Bandini* without losing its trail in the past. Sometimes, lying in bed at night, a phrase or a paragraph or a character from that early work will mesmerize me and in a half dream I will entwine it in phrases and draw from it a kind of melodious memory of an old bedroom in Colorado, or my mother, or my father, or my brothers and sister. I cannot imagine that what I wrote so long ago will soothe me as does this half dream, and yet I cannot bring myself to look back, to open this first novel and read it again. I am fearful, I cannot bear being exposed by my own work. I am sure I shall never read this book again. But of this I am sure: all of the people of my writing life, all of my characters are to be found in this early work. Nothing of myself is there any more, only the memory of old bedrooms, and the sound of my mother's slippers walking to the kitchen.

John Fante

Wait Until Spring,
Bandini

1.

HE CAME ALONG, KICKING THE DEEP SNOW.
Here was a disgusted man. His name was Svevo Bandini,
and he lived three blocks down that street. He was cold and
there were holes in his shoes. That morning he had patched
the holes on the inside with pieces of cardboard from a
macaroni box. The macaroni in that box was not paid for.
He had thought of that as he placed the cardboard inside
of his shoes.

He hated the snow. He was a bricklayer, and the snow
froze the mortar between the brick he laid. He was on his
way home, but what was the sense in going home? When
he was a boy in Italy, in Abruzzi, he hated the snow too.
No sunshine, no work. He was in America now, in the
town of Rocklin, Colorado. He had just been in the Imperial Poolhall. In Italy there were mountains, too, like those
white mountains a few miles west of him. The mountains

were a huge white dress dropped plumb-like to the earth. Twenty years before, when he was twenty years old, he had starved for a full week in the folds of that savage white dress. He had been building a fireplace in a mountain lodge. It was dangerous up there in the winter. He had said the devil with the danger, because he was only twenty then, and he had a girl in Rocklin, and he needed money. But the roof of the lodge had caved beneath the suffocating snow.

It harassed him always, that beautiful snow. He could never understand why he didn't go to California. Yet he stayed in Colorado, in the deep snow, because it was too late now. The beautiful white snow was like the beautiful white wife of Svevo Bandini, so white, so fertile, lying in a white bed in a house up the street. 456 Walnut Street, Rocklin, Colorado.

Svevo Bandini's eyes watered in the cold air. They were brown, they were soft, they were a woman's eyes. At birth he had stolen them from his mother—for after the birth of Svevo Bandini, his mother was never quite the same, always ill, always with sickly eyes after his birth, and then she died and it was Svevo's turn to carry soft brown eyes.

A hundred and fifty pounds was the weight of Svevo Bandini, and he had a son named Arturo who loved to touch his round shoulders and feel for the snakes inside. He was a fine man, Svevo Bandini, all muscles, and he had a wife named Maria who had only to think of the muscle in his loins and her body and her mind melted like the spring snows. She was so white, that Maria, and looking at her was seeing her through a film of olive oil.

Dio cane. Dio cane. It means God is a dog, and Svevo Bandini was saying it to the snow. Why did Svevo lose ten dollars in a poker game tonight at the Imperial Poolhall? He was such a poor man, and he had three children, and the macaroni was not paid, nor was the house in which the three children and the macaroni were kept. God is a dog.

Svevo Bandini had a wife who never said: give me money for food for the children, but he had a wife with large black eyes, sickly bright from love, and those eyes had a way about them, a sly way of peering into his mouth, into his ears, into his stomach, and into his pockets. Those eyes were so clever in a sad way, for they always knew when the Imperial Poolhall had done a good business. Such eyes for a wife! They saw all he was and all he hoped to be, but they never saw his soul.

That was an odd thing, because Maria Bandini was a woman who looked upon all the living and the dead as souls. Maria knew what a soul was. A soul was an immortal thing she knew about. A soul was an immortal thing she would not argue about. A soul was an immortal thing. Well, whatever it was, a soul was immortal.

Maria had a white rosary, so white you could drop it in

the snow and lose it forever, and she prayed for the soul of Svevo Bandini and her children. And because there was no time, she hoped that somewhere in this world someone, a nun in some quiet convent, someone, anyone, found time to pray for the soul of Maria Bandini.

He had a white bed waiting for him, in which his wife lay, warm and waiting, and he was kicking the snow and thinking of something he was going to invent some day. Just an idea he had in his head: a snow plow. He had made a miniature of it out of cigar boxes. He had an idea there. And then he shuddered as you do when cold metal touches your flank, and he was suddenly remembering the many times he had got into the warm bed beside Maria, and the tiny cold cross on her rosary touched his flesh on winter nights like a tittering little cold serpent, and how he withdrew quickly to an even colder part of the bed, and then he thought of the bedroom, of the house that was not paid for, of the white wife endlessly waiting for passion, and he could not endure it, and straightway in his fury he plunged into deeper snow off the sidewalk, letting his anger fight it out with the snow. *Dio cane. Dio cane.*

He had a son named Arturo, and Arturo was fourteen and owned a sled. As he turned into the yard of his house that was not paid for, his feet suddenly raced for the tops of the trees, and he was lying on his back, and Arturo's sled was still in motion, sliding into a clump of snow-weary lilac bushes. *Dio cane!* He had told that boy, that little bastard, to keep his sled out of the front walk. Svevo Bandini felt the snow's cold attacking his hands like frantic ants. He got to his feet, raised his eyes to the sky, shook his fist at God, and nearly collapsed with fury. That Arturo. That little bastard! He dragged the sled from beneath the lilac bush and with systematic fiendishness tore the runners off. Only when the destruction was complete did he remember that the sled had cost seven-fifty. He stood brushing the snow from his clothes, that strange hot feeling in his ankles, where the snow had entered from the tops of his shoes. Seven dollars and fifty cents torn to pieces. *Diavolo!* Let the boy buy another sled. He preferred a new one anyway.

The house was not paid for. It was his enemy, that house. It had a voice, and it was always talking to him, parrot-like, forever chattering the same thing. Whenever his feet made the porch floor creak, the house said insolently: you do not own me, Svevo Bandini, and I will never belong to you. Whenever he touched the front doorknob it was the same. For fifteen years that house had heckled him and exasperated him with its idiotic independence. There were times when he wanted to set dynamite under it, and blow it to pieces. Once it had been a challenge, that house so like a woman, taunting him to possess her. But in thirteen years he had wearied and weakened, and the house had gained in its arrogance. Svevo Bandini no longer cared.

The banker who owned that house was one of his worst enemies. The mental image of that banker's face made his heart pound with a hunger to consume itself in violence. Helmer, the banker. The dirt of the earth. Time and again he had been forced to stand before Helmer and say that he had not enough money to feed his family. Helmer, with the neatly parted grey hair, with the soft hands, the banker eyes that looked like oysters when Svevo Bandini said he had no money to pay the installment on his house. He had had to do that many times, and the soft hands of Helmer unnerved him. He could not talk to that kind of a man. He hated Helmer. He would like to break Helmer's neck, to tear out Helmer's heart and jump on it with both feet. Of Helmer he would think and mutter : the day is coming ! the day is coming ! It was not his house, and he had but to touch the knob to remember it did not belong to him.

Her name was Maria, and the darkness was light before her black eyes. He tiptoed to the corner and a chair there, near the window with the green shade down. When he seated himself both knees clicked. It was like the tinkling of two bells to Maria, and he thought how foolish for a wife to love a man so much. The room was so cold. Funnels of vapor tumbled from his breathing lips. He grunted like a wrestler with his shoe laces. Always trouble with his shoe laces. *Diavolo!* Would he be an old man on his death bed before he ever learned to tie his shoe laces like other men?

"Svevo?"

"Yes."

"Don't break them, Svevo. Turn on the light and I'll untie them. Don't get mad and break them."

God in heaven! Sweet Mother Mary! Wasn't that just like a woman? Get mad? What was there to get mad about? Oh God, he felt like smashing his fist through that window! He gnawed with his fingernails at the knot of his shoe laces. Shoe laces! Why did there have to be shoe laces? Unnh. Unnh. Unnh.

"Svevo."

"Yes."

"I'll do it. Turn on the light."

When the cold has hypnotized your fingers, a knotted thread is as obstinate as barbed wire. With the might of his arm and shoulder he vented his impatience. The lace broke with a cluck sound, and Svevo Bandini almost fell out of the chair. He sighed, and so did his wife.

"Ah, Svevo. You've broken them again."

"Bah," he said. "Do you expect me to go to bed with my shoes on?"

He slept naked, he despised underclothing, but once a year, with the first flurry of snow, he always found long underwear laid out for him on the chair in the corner.

Once he had sneered at this protection: that was the year he had almost died of influenza and pneumonia; that was the winter when he had risen from a death bed, delirious with fever, disgusted with pills and syrups, and staggered to the pantry, choked down his throat a half dozen garlic bulbs, and returned to bed to sweat it out with death. Maria believed her prayers had cured him, and thereafter his religion of cures was garlic, but Maria maintained that garlic came from God, and that was too pointless for Svevo Bandini to dispute.

He was a man, and he hated the sight of himself in long underwear. She was Maria, and every blemish on his underwear, every button and every thread, every odor and every touch, made the points of her breasts ache with a joy that came out of the middle of the earth. They had been married fifteen years, and he had a tongue and spoke well and often of this and that, but rarely had he ever said, I love you. She was his wife, and she spoke rarely, but she tired him often with her constant, I love you.

He walked to the bedside, pushed his hands beneath the covers, and groped for that wandering rosary. Then he slipped between the blankets and seized her frantically, his arms pinioned around hers, his legs locked around hers. It was not passion, it was only the cold of a winter night, and she was a small stove of a woman whose sadness and warmth had attracted him from the first. Fifteen winters, night upon night, and a woman warm and welcoming to her body feet like ice, hands and arms like ice; he thought of such love and sighed.

And a little while ago the Imperial Poolhall had taken his last ten dollars. If only this woman had some fault to cast a hiding shadow upon his own weaknesses. Take Teresa DeRenzo. He would have married Teresa DeRenzo, except that she was extravagant, she talked too much, and her breath smelled like a sewer, and she—a strong, muscular woman—liked to pretend watery weakness in his arms: to think of it! And Teresa DeRenzo was taller than he! Well, with a wife like Teresa he could enjoy giving the Imperial Poolhall ten dollars in a poker game. He could think of that breath, that chattering mouth, and he could thank God for a chance to waste his hard-earned money. But not Maria.

"Arturo broke the kitchen window," she said.

"Broke it? How?"

"He pushed Federico's head through it."

"The son of a bitch."

"He didn't mean it. He was only playing."

"And what did you do? Nothing, I suppose."

"I put iodine on Federico's head. A little cut. Nothing serious."

"Nothing serious! Whaddya mean, nothing serious! What'd you do to Arturo?"

"He was mad. He wanted to go to the show."

"And he went."

"Kids like shows."

"The dirty little son of a bitch."

"Svevo, why talk like that? Your own son."

"You've spoiled him. You've spoiled them all."

"He's like you Svevo. You were a bad boy too."

"I was—like hell! You didn't catch me pushing my brother's head through a window."

"You didn't have any brothers, Svevo. But you pushed your father down the steps and broke his arm."

"Could I help it if my father . . . Oh, forget it."

He wriggled closer and pushed his face into her braided hair. Ever since the birth of August, their third son, his wife's right ear had an odor of chloroform. She had brought it home from the hospital with her ten years ago: or was it his imagination? He had quarreled with her about this for years, for she always denied there was a chloroform odor in her right ear. Even the children had experimented, and they had failed to smell it. Yet it was there, always there, just as it was that night in the ward, when he bent down to kiss her, after she had come out of it, so near death, yet alive.

"What if I did push my father down the steps? What's that got to do with it?"

"Did it spoil you? Are you spoiled?"

"How do I know?"

"You're not spoiled."

What the hell kind of thinking was that? Of course he was spoiled! Teresa DeRenzo had always told him he was vicious and selfish and spoiled. It used to delight him. And that girl—what was her name—Carmela, Carmela Ricci, the friend of Rocco Saccone, she thought he was a devil, and she was wise, she had been through college, the University of Colorado, a college graduate, and she had said he was a wonderful scoundrel, cruel, dangerous, a menace to young women. But Maria—oh Maria, she thought he was an angel, pure as bread. Bah. What did Maria know about it? She had had no college education, why she had not even finished high school.

Not even high school. Her name was Maria Bandini, but before she married him her name was Maria Toscana, and she never finished high school. She was the youngest daughter in a family of two girls and a boy. Tony and Teresa—both high school graduates. But Maria? The family curse was upon her, this lowest of all the Toscanas, this girl who wanted things her own way and refused to graduate from high school. The ignorant Toscana. The one without a high school diploma—almost a diploma, three and one-half years, but still, no diploma. Tony and Teresa had them, and Carmela Ricci, the friend of Rocco, had even gone to the University of Colorado. God was against him. Of them all, why had he fallen in love with this woman at his side, this woman without a high school diploma?

"Christmas will soon be here, Svevo," she said. "Say a prayer. Ask God to make it a happy Christmas."

Her name was Maria, and she was always telling him something he already knew. Didn't he know without being told that Christmas would soon be here? Here it was, the night of December fifth. When a man goes to sleep beside his wife on a Thursday night, is it necessary for her to tell him the next day would be Friday? And that boy Arturo—why was he cursed with a son who played with a sled? *Ah, povera America!* And he should pray for a happy Christmas. Bah.

"Are you warm enough, Svevo?"

There she was, always wanting to know if he was warm enough. She was a little over five feet tall, and he never knew whether she was sleeping or waking, she was that quiet. A wife like a ghost, always content in her little half of the bed, saying the rosary and praying for a merry Christmas. Was it any wonder that he couldn't pay for this house, this mad-house occupied by a wife who was a religious fanatic? A man needed a wife to goad him on, inspire him, and make him work hard. But Maria? *Ah, povera America!*

She slipped from her side of the bed, her toes with sure precision found the slippers on the rug in the darkness, and he knew she was going to the bathroom first, and to inspect the boys afterward, the final inspection before she returned to bed for the rest of the night. A wife who was always slipping out of bed to look at her three sons. Ah, such a life! *Io sono fregato!*

How could a man get any sleep in this house, always in a turmoil, his wife always getting out of bed without a word? Goddamn the Imperial Poolhall! A full house, queens on deuces, and he had lost. *Madonna!* And he should pray for a happy Christmas! With that kind of luck he should even talk to God! *Jesu Christi,* if God really existed, let Him answer—why!

As quietly as she had gone, she was beside him again.

"Federico has a cold," she said.

He too had a cold—in his soul. His son Federico could have a snivel and Maria would rub menthol on his chest, and lie there half the night talking about it, but Svevo Bandini suffered alone—not with an aching body: worse, with an aching soul. Where upon the earth was the pain greater than in your own soul? Did Maria help him? Did she ever ask him if he suffered from the hard times? Did she ever say, Svevo, my beloved, how is your soul these days? Are you happy, Svevo? Is there any chance for work this winter, Svevo? *Dio Maledetto!* And she wanted a merry Christmas! How can you have a merry Christmas when you are alone among three sons and a wife? Holes in your shoes, bad luck at cards, no work, break your neck on a goddamn sled—and you want a merry Christmas! Was he a millionaire? He might have been, if he had married the right kind of woman. Heh: he was too stupid though.

Her name was Maria, and he felt the softness of the bed recede beneath him, and he had to smile for he knew she was coming nearer, and his lips opened a little to receive them—three fingers of a small hand, touching his lips, lifting him to a warm land inside the sun, and then she was blowing her breath faintly into his nostrils from pouted lips.

"*Cara sposa,*" he said. "Dear wife."

Her lips were wet and she rubbed them against his eyes. He laughed softly.

"I'll kill you," he whispered.

She laughed, then listened, poised, listened for a sound of the boys awake in the next room.

"*Che sara, sara,*" she said. "What must be, must be."

Her name was Maria, and she was so patient, waiting for him, touching the muscle at his loins, so patient, kissing him here and there, and then the great heat he loved consumed him and she lay back.

"Ah, Svevo. So wonderful!"

He loved her with such gentle fierceness, so proud of himself, thinking all the time: she is not so foolish, this Maria, she knows what is good. The big bubble they chased toward the sun exploded between them, and he groaned with joyous release, groaned like a man glad he had been able to forget for a little while so many things, and Maria, very quiet in her little half of the bed, listened to the pounding of her heart and wondered how much he had lost at the Imperial Poolhall. A great deal, no doubt; possibly ten dollars, for Maria had no high school diploma but she could read that man's misery in meter of his passion.

"Svevo," she whispered.

But he was sound asleep.

Bandini, hater of snow. He leaped out of bed at five that morning, like a skyrocket out of bed, making ugly faces at the cold morning, sneering at it: bah, this Colorado, the rear end of God's creation, always frozen, no place for an Italian bricklayer; ah, he was cursed with this life. On the sides of his feet he walked to the chair and snatched his pants and shoved his legs through them, thinking he was losing twelve dollars a day, union scale, eight hours hard work, and all because of that! He jerked the curtain string; it shot up and rattled like a machine gun, and the white naked morning dove into the room, splashing brightly over him. He growled at it. *Sporca chone*: dirty face, he called it. *Sporcaccione ubriaco*: drunken dirty face.

Maria slept with the drowsy awareness of a kitten, and that curtain brought her awake quickly, her eyes in nimble terror.

"Svevo. It's too early."

"Go to sleep. Who's asking you? Go to sleep."

"What time is it?"

"Time for a man to get up. Time for a woman to go to sleep. Shut up."

She had never got used to this early morning rising. Seven was her hour, not counting the times in the hospital, and once, she had stayed in bed until nine, and got a headache because of it, but this man she had married always shot out of bed at five in winter, and at six in summer. She knew his torment in the white prison of winter; she knew that when she arose in two hours he would have shoveled every clod of snow from every path in and around the yard, half a block down the street, under the clothes lines, far down the alley, piling it high, moving it around, cutting it viciously with his flat shovel.

And it was so. When she got up and slipped her feet inside of slippers, the toes aburst like frayed flowers, she looked through the kitchen window and saw where he was, out there in the alley, beyond the high fence. A giant of a man, a dwarfed giant hidden on the other side of a six foot fence, his shovel peering over the top now and then, throwing puffs of snow back to the sky.

But he had not built a fire in the kitchen stove. Oh no, he never built a fire in the kitchen stove. What was he—a woman, that he should build a fire? Sometimes though. Once he had taken them into the mountains for a beefsteak fry, and absolutely no one but himself was permitted to build that fire. But a kitchen stove! What was he—a woman?

It was so cold that morning, so cold. Her jaw chattered and ran away from her. The dark green linoleum might have been a sheet of ice under her feet, the stove itself a block of ice. What a stove that was! a despot, untamed and ill-tempered. She always coaxed it, soothed it, cajoled it, a black bear of a stove subject to fits of rebellion, defying Maria to make him glow; a cantankerous stove that, once warm and pouring sweet heat, suddenly went berserk and got yellow hot and threatened to destroy the very house. Only Maria could handle that black block of sulking iron, and she did it a twig at a time, caressing the shy flame, adding a slab of wood, then another and another, until it purred beneath her care, the iron heating up, the oven expanding and the heat thumping it until it grunted and groaned in content, like an idiot. She was Maria, and the stove loved only her. Let Arturo or August drop a lump of coal into its greedy mouth and it went mad with its own fever, burning and blistering the paint on the walls, turning a frightful yellow, a chunk of hell hissing for Maria, who came frowning and capable, a cloth in her hand as she twitted it here and there, shutting the vents deftly, shaking its bowels until it resumed its stupid normalcy. Maria, with hands no larger than frayed roses, but that black devil was her slave, and she really was very fond of it. She kept it shining and flashily vicious, its nickel plated trade name grinning evilly like a mouth too proud of its beautiful teeth.

When at length the flames rose and it groaned good morning, she put water on for coffee and returned to the window. Svevo was in the chicken yard, panting as he leaned on his shovel. The hens had come out of the shed, clucking as they eyed him, this man who could lift the fallen white heavens off the ground and throw them over the fence. But from the window she saw that the hens did not saunter too close to him. She knew why. They were her hens; they ate from her hands, but they hated him; they remembered him as the one who sometimes came of a Saturday night to kill. This was alright; they were very grateful he had shoveled the snow away so they could scratch the earth, they appreciated it, but they could never trust him as they did the woman who came with corn dripping from her small hands. And spaghetti too, in a dish; they kissed her with their beaks when she brought them spaghetti; but beware of this man.

Their names were Arturo, August, and Federico. They were awake now, their eyes all brown and bathed brightly in the black river of sleep. They were all in one bed, Arturo twelve, August ten, and Federico eight. Italian boys, fooling around, three in a bed, laughing the quick peculiar laugh of obscenity. Arturo, he knew plenty. He was telling them now what he knew, the words coming from his mouth in hot white vapor in the cold room. He knew plenty. He had seen plenty. He knew plenty. You guys don't know what I saw. She was sitting on the porch steps. I was about this far from her. I saw plenty.

Federico, eight years old.

"What'ya see, Arturo?"

"Shut yer mouth, ya little sap. We ain't talkin' to you!"

"I won't tell, Arturo."

"Ah, shut yer mouth. You're too little!"

"I'll tell, then."

They joined forces then, and threw him out of bed. He bumped against the floor, whimpering. The cold air seized him with a sudden fury and pricked him with ten thousand needles. He screamed and tried to get under the covers again, but they were stronger than he and he dashed around the bed and into his mother's room. She was pulling on her cotton stockings. He was screaming with dismay.

"They kicked me out! Arturo did. August did!"

"Snitcher!" yelled from the next room.

He was so beautiful to her, that Federico; his skin was so beautiful to her. She took him into her arms and rubbed her hands into his back, pinching his beautiful little bottom, squeezing him hard, pushing heat into him, and he thought of the odor of her, wondering what it was and how good it was in the morning.

"Sleep in Mamma's bed," she said.

He climbed in quickly, and she clamped the covers around him, shaking him with delight, and he was so glad he was on Mamma's side of the bed, with his head in the nest Mamma's hair made, because he didn't like Papa's pillow; it was kind of sour and strong, but Mamma's smelt sweet and made him warm all over.

"I know somethin' else," Arturo said. "But I ain't telling."

August was ten; he didn't know much. Of course he knew more than his punk brother Federico, but not half so much as the brother beside him, Arturo, who knew plenty about women and stuff.

"What'll ya give me if I tell ya?" Arturo said.

"Give you a milk nickel."

"Milk nickel! What the heck! Who wants a milk nickel in winter?"

"Give it to you next summer."

"Nuts to you. What'll ya give me now?"

"Give you anything I got."

"It's a bet. Whatcha got?"

"Ain't got nothing."

"Okay. I ain't telling nothing, then."

"You ain't got anything to tell."

"Like hell I haven't!"

"Tell me for nothing."

"Nothing doing."

"You're lying, that's why. You're a liar."

"Don't call me a liar!"

"You're a liar if you don't tell. Liar!"

He was Arturo, and he was fourteen. He was a miniature of his father, without the mustache. His upper lip curled with such gentle cruelty. Freckles swarmed over his face like ants over a piece of cake. He was the oldest, and he thought he was pretty tough, and no sap kid brother could call him a liar and get away with it. In five seconds August was writhing. Arturo was under the covers at his brother's feet.

"That's my toe hold," he said.

"Ow! Leggo!"

"Who's a liar!"

"Nobody!"

Their mother was Maria, but they called her Mamma, and she was beside them now, still frightened at the duty of motherhood, still mystified by it. There was August now; it was easy to be his mother. He had yellow hair, and a hundred times a day, out of nowhere at all, there came that thought, that her second son had yellow hair. She could kiss August at will, lean down and taste the yellow hair and press her mouth on his face and eyes. He was a good boy, August was. Of course, she had had a lot of trouble with him. Weak kidneys, Doctor Hewson had said, but that was over now, and the mattress was never wet anymore in the mornings. August would grow up to be a fine man now, never wetting the bed. A hundred nights she had spent on her knees at his side while he slept, her rosary beads clicking in the dark as she prayed God, please Blessed Lord, don't let my son wet the bed anymore. A hundred, two hundred nights. The doctor had called it weak kidneys; she had called it God's will; and Svevo Bandini had called it god-damn carelessness and was in favor of making August sleep in the chicken yard, yellow hair or no yellow hair. There had been all sorts of suggestions for cure. The doctor kept prescribing pills. Svevo was in favor of the razor strap, but she had always tricked him out of the idea; and her own mother, Donna Toscana had insisted that August drink his own urine. But her name was Maria, and so was the Savior's mother, and she had gone to that other Maria over miles and miles of rosary beads. Well, August had stopped, hadn't he? When she slipped her hand under him in the early hours of the morning, wasn't he dry and warm? And why? Maria knew why. Nobody else could explain it. Bandini had said, by God it's about time; the doctor had said it was the pills had done it, and Donna Toscana insisted it would have stopped a long time ago had they followed her suggestion. Even August was amazed and delighted on those mornings when he wakened to find himself dry and clean. He could remember those nights when he woke up to find his mother on her knees beside him,

her face against his, the beads ticking, her breath in his
nostrils and the whispered little words, Hail Mary, Hail
Mary, poured into his nose and eyes until he felt an eerie
melancholy as he lay between these two women, a help-
lessness that choked him and made him determined to
please them both. He simply *wouldn't* pee the bed again.

It was easy to be the mother of August. She could play
with the yellow hair whenever she pleased because he was
filled with the wonder and mystery of her. She had done
so much for him, that Maria. She had made him grow up.
She had made him feel like a real boy, and no longer could
Arturo tease him and hurt him because of his weak kidneys.
When she came on whispering feet to his bedside each
night he had only to feel the warm fingers caressing his
hair, and he was reminded again that she and another
Maria had changed him from a sissy to a real guy. No
wonder she smelled so good. And Maria never forgot the
wonder of that yellow hair. Where it came from God only
knew, and she was so proud of it.

Breakfast for three boys and a man. His name was Arturo,
but he hated it and wanted to be called John. His last name
was Bandini, and he wanted it to be Jones. His mother and
father were Italians, but he wanted to be an American. His
father was a bricklayer, but he wanted to be a pitcher for
the Chicago Cubs. They lived in Rocklin, Colorado, popula-
tion ten thousand, but he wanted to live in Denver, thirty

miles away. His face was freckled, but he wanted it to be clear. He went to a Catholic school, but he wanted to go to a public school. He had a girl named Rosa, but she hated him. He was an altar boy, but he was a devil and hated altar boys. He wanted to be a good boy, but he was afraid to be a good boy because he was afraid his friends would call him a good boy. He was Arturo and he loved his father, but he lived in dread of the day when he would grow up and be able to lick his father. He worshipped his father, but he thought his mother was a sissy and a fool.

Why was his mother unlike other mothers? She was that, and everyday he saw it again. Jack Hawley's mother excited him: she had a way of handing him cookies that made his heart purr. Jim Toland's mother had bright legs. Carl Molla's mother never wore anything but a gingham dress; when she swept the floor of the Molla kitchen he stood on the back porch in an ecstasy, watching Mrs. Molla sweep, his hot eyes gulping the movement of her hips. He was twelve, and the realization that his mother did not excite him made him hate her secretly. Always out of the corner of his eye he watched his mother. He loved his mother, but he hated her.

Why did his mother permit Bandini to boss her? Why was she afraid of him? When they were in bed and he lay awake sweating in hatred, why did his mother let Bandini do that to her? When she left the bathroom and came into the boys' bedroom, why did she smile in the darkness ? He could not see her smile, but he knew it was upon her face, that content of the night, so much in love with the darkness and hidden lights warming her face. Then he hated them both, but his hatred of her was greatest. He felt like spitting on her, and long after she had returned to bed the hatred was upon his face, the muscles in his cheeks weary with it.

Breakfast was ready. He could hear his father asking for coffee. Why did his father have to yell all the time ? Couldn't he talk in a low voice ? Everybody in the neighborhood knew everything that went on in their house on account of his father constantly shouting. The Moreys next door— you never heard a peep out of them, never ; quiet, American people. But his father wasn't satisfied with being an Italian, he had to be a noisy Italian.

"Arturo," his mother called. "Breakfast."

As if he didn't know breakfast was ready! As if everybody in Colorado didn't know by this time that the Bandini family was having breakfast!

He hated soap and water, and he could never understand why you had to wash your face every morning. He hated the bathroom because there was no bathtub in it. He hated toothbrushes. He hated the toothpaste his mother bought. He hated the family comb, always clogged with mortar from his father's hair, and he loathed his own hair because it never stayed down. Above all, he hated his own face spotted with freckles like ten thousand pennies poured over a rug. The only thing about the bathroom he liked was the loose floorboard in the corner. Here he hid *Scarlet Crime* and *Terror Tales.*

"Arturo! Your eggs are getting cold."

Eggs. Oh Lord, how he hated eggs.

They were cold, alright; but no colder than the eyes of his father, who glared at him as he sat down. Then he remembered, and a glance told him that his mother had snitched. Oh Jesus! To think that his own mother should rat on him! Bandini nodded to the window with eight panes across the room, one pane gone, the opening covered with a dish towel.

"So you pushed your brother's head through the window?"

It was too much for Federico. All over again he saw it: Arturo angry, Arturo pushing him into the window, the crash of glass. Suddenly Federico began to cry. He had not cried last night, but now he remembered: blood coming out of his hair, his mother washing the wound, telling him to be brave. It was awful. Why hadn't he cried last night? He couldn't remember, but he was crying now, the knuckle of his fist twisting tears out of his eyes.

"Shut up!" Bandini said.

"Let somebody push *your* head through a window," Federico sobbed. "See if *you* don't cry!"

Arturo loathed him. Why did he have to have a little brother? Why had he stood in front of the window? What kind of people were these Wops? Look at his father, there. Look at him smashing eggs with his fork to show how angry he was. Look at the egg yellow on his father's chin! And on his mustache. Oh sure, he was a Dago Wop, so he had to have a mustache, but did he have to pour those eggs through his ears? Couldn't he find his mouth? Oh God, these Italians!

But Federico was quiet now. His martyrdom of last night no longer interested him; he had found a crumb of bread in his milk, and it reminded him of a boat floating on the ocean; *Drrrrrrr*, said the motor boat, *drrrrrrr*. What if the ocean was made out of real milk—could you get ice cream at the North Pole? *Drrrrrrr*, *drrrrrrr*. Suddenly he was thinking of last night again. A gusher of tears filled his eyes and he sobbed. But the bread crumb was sinking. *Drrrrrr*, *drrrrr*. Don't sink, motor boat! don't sink! Bandini was watching him.

"For Christ's sake!" he said. "Will you drink that milk and quit fooling around?"

To use the name of Christ carelessly was like slapping Maria across the mouth. When she married Bandini it had not occurred to her that he swore. She never quite got used to it. But Bandini swore at everything. The first English words he learned were God damn it. He was very proud of his swear words. When he was furious he always relieved himself in two languages.

"Well," he said. "Why did you push your brother's head through the window?"

"How do I know?" Arturo said. "I just did it, that's all."

Bandini rolled his eyes in horror.

"And how do you know I won't knock your goddamn block off?"

"Svevo," Maria said. "Svevo. Please."

"What do *you* want?" he said.

"He didn't mean it, Svevo," she smiled. "It was an accident. Boys will be boys."

He put down his napkin with a bang. He clinched his teeth and seized the hair on his head with both hands. There he swayed in his chair, back and forth, back and forth.

"Boys will be boys!" he jibed. "That little bastard pushes his brother's head through the window, and boys will be boys! Who's gonna pay for that window? Who's gonna pay the doctor bills when he pushes his brother off a cliff? Who's gonna pay the lawyer when they send him to jail for murdering his brother? A murderer in the family! *Oh Deo uta me!* Oh God help me!"

Maria shook her head and smiled. Arturo screwed his lips in a murderous sneer: so his own father was against him too, already accusing him of murder. August's head racked sadly, but he was very happy that he wasn't going to turn out to be a murderer like his brother Arturo; as for August he was going to be a priest; maybe he would be there to deliver the last sacraments before they sent Arturo to the electric chair. As for Federico, he saw himself the victim of his brother's passion, saw himself lying stretched out at the funeral; all his friends from St. Catherine were there, kneeling and crying; oh, it was awful. His eyes floated once more, and he sobbed bitterly, wondering if he could have another glass of milk.

"Kin I have a motor boat for Christmas?" he said.

Bandini glared at him, astonished.

"That's all we need in this family," he said. Then his tongue flitted sarcastically: "Do you want a real motor boat, Federico? One that goes put put pt put?"

"That's what I want!" Federico laughed. "One that goes puttedy puttedy put put!" He was already in it, steering it over the kitchen table and across Blue Lake up in the mountains. Bandini's leer caused him to kill the motor and drop anchor. He was very quiet now. Bandini's leer was steady, straight through him. Federico wanted to cry again, but he didn't dare. He dropped his eyes to the empty milk glass, saw a drop or two at the bottom of the glass, and drained them carefully, his eyes stealing a glance at his father over the top of the glass. There sat Svevo Bandini—leering. Federico felt goose flesh creeping over him.

"Gee whiz," he whimpered. "What did *I* do?"

It broke the silence. They all relaxed, even Bandini, who had held the scene long enough. Quietly he spoke.

"No motor boats, understand? Absolutely no motor boats."

Was that all? Federico sighed happily. And all the time he believed his father had discovered that it was he who had stolen the pennies out of his work pants, broken the street lamp on the corner, drawn that picture of Sister Mary Constance on the blackboard, hit Stella Colombo in the eye with a snowball, and spat in the holy water font at St. Catherine's.

Sweetly he said, "I don't want a motor boat, Papa. If you don't want me to have one, I don't want one, Papa."

Bandini nodded self-approvingly to his wife: here was the way to raise children, his nod said. When you want a kid to do something, just stare at him; that's the way to raise a boy. Arturo cleaned the last of his egg from the plate and sneered: Jesus, what a sap his old man was! He knew that Federico, Arturo did; he knew what a dirty little crook Federico was; that sweet face stuff wasn't fooling him by a long shot, and suddenly he wished he had shoved not only Federico's head but his whole body, head and feet and all, through that window.

"When I was a boy," Bandini began. "When I was a boy back in the Old Country—"

At once Federico and Arturo left the table. This was old

stuff to them. They knew he was going to tell them for the ten thousandth time that he made four cents a day carrying stone on his back, when he was a boy, back in the Old Country, carrying stone on his back, when he was a boy. The story hypnotized Svevo Bandini. It was dream stuff that suffocated and blurred Helmer the banker, holes in his shoes, a house that was not paid for, and children that must be fed. When I was a boy: dream stuff. The progression of years, the crossing of an ocean, the accumulation of mouths to feed, the heaping of trouble upon trouble, year upon year, was something to boast about too, like the gathering of great wealth. He could not buy shoes with it, but it had happened to him. When I was a boy—. Maria, listening once more, wondered why he always put it that way, always deferring to the years, making himself old.

A letter from Donna Toscana arrived, Maria's mother. Donna Toscana with the big red tongue, not big enough to check the flow of angry saliva at the very thought of her daughter married to Svevo Bandini. Maria turned the letter over and over. The flap gushed glue thickly where Donna's huge tongue had mopped it. Maria Toscana, 345 Walnut Street, Rocklin, Colorado, for Donna refused to use the married name of her daughter. The heavy, savage writing might have been streaks from a hawk's bleeding beak, the script of a peasant woman who had just slit a goat's throat. Maria did not open the letter; she knew its substance.

Bandini entered from the back yard. In his hands he carried a heavy lump of bright coal. He dropped it into the coal bucket behind the stove. His hands were smeared with black dust. He frowned; to carry coal disgusted him; it was a woman's work. He looked irritably at Maria. She nodded to the letter propped against a battered salt cellar on the yellow oil cloth. The heavy writing of his mother-in-law writhed like tiny serpents before his eyes. He hated Donna Toscana with a fury that amounted to fear. They clashed like male and female animals whenever they met. It gave him pleasure to seize that letter in his blackened, grimy hands. It delighted him to tear it open raggedly, with no care for the message inside. Before he read the script he lifted piercing eyes to his wife, to let her know once more how deeply he hated the woman who had given her life. Maria was helpless; this was not her quarrel, all of her married life she had ignored it, and she would have destroyed the letter had not Bandini forbidden her even to open messages from her mother. He got a vicious pleasure out of her mother's letters that was quite horrifying to Maria; there was something black and terrible about it, like peering under a damp stone. It was the diseased pleasure of a martyr, of a man who got an almost exotic joy out of the castigation of a mother-in-law who enjoyed his misery now that he had come upon hard times. Bandini loved it, that persecution, for it gave him a wild impetus to drunkenness. He

rarely drank to excess because it sickened him, but a letter
from Donna Toscana had a blinding effect upon him. It
served him with a pretext that prescribed oblivion, for when
he was drunk he could hate his mother-in-law to the point of
hysteria, and he could forget, he could forget his house that
remained unpaid, his bills, the pressing monotony of marriage. It meant escape: a day, two days, a week of hypnosis—
and Maria could remember periods when he was drunk
for two weeks. There was no concealing of Donna's letters
from him. They came rarely, but they meant only one
thing; that Donna would spend an afternoon with them.
If she came without his seeing a letter, Bandini knew his
wife had hidden the letter. The last time she did that, Svevo
lost his temper and gave Arturo a terrible beating for putting
too much salt on his macaroni, a meaningless offense, and,
of course, one he would not have noticed under ordinary
circumstances. But the letter had been concealed, and someone had to suffer for it.

This latest letter was dated of the day before, December
8th, the feast of the Immaculate Conception. As Bandini
read the lines, the flesh upon his face whitened and his blood
disappeared like sand swallowing the ebb tide. The letter
read:

> *My Dear Maria:*
> *Today is the glorious feast day of our Blessed Mother,*
> *and I go to Church to pray for you in your misery. My*

heart goes out to you and the poor children, cursed as they are by the tragic condition in which you live. I have asked the Blessed Mother to have mercy on you, and to bring happiness to those little ones who do not deserve their fate. I will be in Rocklin Sunday afternoon, and will leave by the eight o'clock bus. All love and sympathy to you and the children.

Donna Toscana.

Without looking at his wife, Bandini put the letter down and began gnawing at an already ravaged thumb nail. His fingers plucked his lower lip. His fury began somewhere outside of him. She could feel it rising from the corners of the room, from the walls and the floor, an odor moving in a whirlpool completely outside of herself. Simply to distract herself, she straightened her blouse.

Feebly she said, "Now, Svevo—"

He arose, chucked her under the chin, his lips smiling fiendishly to inform her that this show of affection was not sincere, and walked out of the room.

"Oh Marie!" he sang, no music in his voice, only hatred pushing a lyrical love song out of his throat. "Oh Marie. Oh Marie! *Quanto sonna perdato per te! Fa me dor me! Fa me dor me!* Oh Marie, Oh Marie! How much sleep I have lost because of you! Oh let me sleep, my darling Marie!"

There was no stopping him. She listened to his feet on

thin soles as they flecked the floor like drops of water spitting on a stove. She heard the swish of his patched and sewed overcoat as he flung himself into it. Then silence for a moment, until she heard a match strike, and she knew he was lighting a cigar. His fury was too great for her. To interfere would have been to give him the temptation of knocking her down. As his steps approached the front door, she held her breath: there was a glass panel in that front door. But no—he closed it quietly and was gone. In a little while now he would meet his good friend, Rocco Saccone, the stonecutter, the only human being she really hated. Rocco Saccone, the boyhood friend of Svevo Bandini, the whiskey-drinking bachelor who had tried to prevent Bandini's marriage; Rocco Saccone, who wore white flannels in all seasons and boasted disgustingly of his Saturday night seductions of married American women at the Old-time dances up in the Odd Fellows Hall. She could trust Svevo. He would float his brains on a sea of whiskey, but he would not be unfaithful to her. She knew that. But could she? With a gasp she threw herself into the chair by the table and wept as she buried her face in her hands.

2.

IT WAS A QUARTER TO THREE IN THE EIGHTH
Grade Room at St. Catherine's. Sister Mary Celia, her glass
eye aching in its socket, was in a dangerous mood. The left
eyelid kept twitching, completely out of control. Twenty
eighth graders, eleven boys and nine girls, watched the
twitching eyelid. A quarter to three: fifteen minutes to go.
Nellie Doyle, her thin dress caught between her buttocks,
was reciting the economic effects of Eli Whitney's cotton
gin, and two boys behind her, Jim Lacey and Eddie Holm,
were laughing like hell, only not out loud, at the dress
caught in Nellie's buttocks. They had been told time and
time again to watch out, if the lid over Old Celia's glass eye
started jumping, but would you look at Doyle there!

"The economic effects of Eli Whitney's cotton gin were
unprecedented in the history of cotton," Nellie said.

Sister Mary Celia rose to her feet.

"Holm and Lacey!" she demanded. "Stand up!"

Nellie sat down in confusion, and the two boys got to their feet. Lacey's knees cracked, and the class tittered, Lacey grinned, then blushed. Holm coughed, keeping his head down as he studied the trade lettering on the side of his pencil. It was the first time in his life he had ever read such writing, and he was rather surprised to learn it said simply, Walter Pencil Co.

"Holm and Lacey," Sister Celia said. "I'm bored with grinning goons in my classes. Sit down!" Then she addressed the whole group, but she was really speaking to the boys alone, for the girls rarely gave her trouble: "And the next scoundrel I catch not paying attention to recitation has to stay until six o'clock. Carry on, Nellie."

Nellie stood up again. Lacey and Holm, amazed that they had got off so easy, kept their heads turned toward the other side of the classroom, both afraid they might laugh again if Nellie's dress was still stuck.

"The economic effects of Eli Whitney's cotton gin were unprecedented in the history of cotton," Nellie said.

In a whisper, Lacey spoke to the boy in front of him.

"Hey, Holm. Give the Bandini a gander."

Arturo sat in the opposite side of the room, three desks from the front. His head was low, his chest against the desk, and propped against the ink-stand was a small hand mirror into which he stared as he worked the point of a pencil along the line of his nose. He was counting his freckles. Last night he had slept with his face smeared with lemon juice: it was supposed to be wonderful for the wiping out of freckles. He counted, ninety-three, ninety-four, ninety-five . . . A sense of life's futility occupied him. Here it was, the dead of winter, with the sun showing itself only a moment in the late afternoons, and the count around his nose and cheeks had jumped nine freckles to the grand total of ninety-five. What was the good of living? And last night he had used lemon juice, too. Who was that liar of a woman who had written on the Home Page of yesterday's *Denver Post* that freckles 'fled like the wind' from lemon juice? To be freckled was bad enough, but as far as he knew, he was the only freckle-faced Wop on earth. Where had he got these freckles? From what side of the family had he inherited those little copper marks of the beast? Grimly he began to poll around his left ear. The faint report of the economic effects of Eli Whitney's cotton gin came to him vaguely. Josephine Perlotta was reciting: who the hell cared what Perlotta had to say about the cotton gin? She was a Dago—how could she possibly know anything about cotton gins? In June, thank God for that, he would graduate from this dump of a Catholic school, and enroll in a public high school, where the Wops were few and far between. The count on his left ear was already seventeen, two more than yesterday. God damn these freckles! Now a new voice spoke of the cotton gin, a voice like a soft violin, sending vibrations through his flesh, catching his breath. He put down his pencil and gaped. There she stood in front of him—his beautiful Rosa Pinelli, his love, his girl. Oh you cotton gin! Oh you wonderful Eli Whitney! Oh Rosa, how wonderful you are. I love you, Rosa, I love you, love you, love you!

She was an Italian, sure; but could she help that? Was it her fault anymore than it was his? Oh look at her hair! Look at her shoulders! Look at that pretty green dress! Listen to that voice! Oh you Rosa! Tell 'em Rosa. Tell 'em about that cotton gin! I know you hate me, Rosa. But I love you, Rosa. I love you, and some day you'll see me playing center field for the New York Yanks, Rosa. I'll be out there in center field, Honey, and you'll be my girl, sitting in a box seat off third base, and I'll come in, and it'll be the last half of the ninth, and the Yanks'll be three runs behind. But don't you worry, Rosa! I'll get up there with three men on base, and I'll look at you, and you'll throw me a kiss, and I'll bust that old apple right over the center field wall. I'll make history, Honey. You kiss me and I'll make history!

"Arturo Bandini!"

I won't have any freckles then, either, Rosa. They'll be gone—they always leave when you grow up.

"Arturo Bandini!"

I'll change my name too, Rosa. They'll call me Banning, the Banning Bambino; Art, the Battering Bandit . . .

"Arturo Bandini!"

That time he heard it. The roar of the World Series crowd was gone. He looked up to find Sister Mary Celia looming over her desk, her fist pounding it, her left eye twitching. They were staring at him, all of them, even his Rosa laughing at him, and his stomach rolled out from under him as he realized he had been whispering his fancy aloud. The others could laugh if they pleased, but Rosa—ah Rosa, and her laughter was more poignant than all others, and he felt it hurting him, and he hated her: this Dago girl, daughter of a Wop coal miner who worked in that guinea-town Louisville: a goddamn lousy coal miner. Salvatore was his name; Salvatore Pinelli, so low down he had to work in a coal mine. Could he put up a wall that lasted years and years, a hundred, two hundred years? Nah—the Dago fool, he had a coal pick and a lamp on his cap, and he had to go down under the ground and make his living like a lousy damn Dago rat. His name was Arturo Bandini, and if there was anybody in this school who wanted to make something out of it, let him speak up and get his nose broke.

"Arturo Bandini!"

"Okay," he drawled. "Okay, Sister Celia. I heard you." Then he stood up. The class watched him. Rosa whispered something to the girl behind her, smiling behind her hand. He saw the gesture and he was ready to scream at her, think-

· 50 ·

ing she had made some remark about his freckles, or the big patch on the knee of his pants, or the fact that he needed a hair cut, or the cut down and remodeled shirt his father once wore that never fit him smartly.

"Bandini," Sister Celia said. "You are unquestionably a moron. I warned you about not paying attention. Such stupidity must be rewarded. You're to stay after school until six o'clock."

He sat down, and the three o'clock bell sounded hysterically through the halls.

He was alone, with Sister Celia at her desk, correcting papers. She worked oblivious of him, the left eyelid twitching irritably. In the southwest the pale sun appeared, sickly, more like a weary moon on that winter afternoon. He sat with his chin resting in one hand, watching the cold sun. Beyond the windows the line of fir trees seemed to grow even colder beneath their sad white burdens. Somewhere in the street he heard the shout of a boy, and then the clanking of tire chains. He hated the winter. He could picture the baseball diamond behind the school, buried in snow, the backstop behind home plate cluttered with fantastic heaviness—the whole scene so lonely, so sad. What was there to do in winter? He was almost satisfied to sit there, and his punishment amused him. After all, this was as good a place to sit as anywhere.

"Do you want me to do anything, Sister?" he asked.

Without looking up from her work, she answered, "I want you to sit still and keep quiet—if that's possible."

He smiled and drawled, "Okay, Sister."

He was both still and quiet for all of ten minutes.

"Sister," he said. "Want me to do the blackboards?"

"We pay a man for doing that," she said. "Rather, I should say we overpay a man for that."

"Sister," he said. "Do you like baseball?"

"Football's my game," she said. "I hate baseball. It bores me."

"That's because you don't understand the finer side of the game."

"Quiet, Bandini," she said. "If you please."

He changed his position, resting his chin on his arms and watching her closely. The left eyelid twitched incessantly. He wondered how she had got a glass eye. He had always suspected that someone had hit her with a baseball; now he was almost sure of it. She had come to St. Catherine's from Fort Dodge, Iowa. He wondered what kind of baseball they played in Iowa, and if there were very many Italians there.

"How's your mother?" she asked.

"I don't know. Swell, I guess."

She raised her face from her work for the first time and looked at him. "What do you mean, you *guess*? Don't you know? Your mother's a dear person, a beautiful person. She has the soul of an angel."

As far as he knew, he and his brothers were the only non-paying students at that Catholic school. The tuition was only two dollars a month for each child, but that meant six a month for him and his two brothers, and it was never paid. It was a distinction of great torment to him, this feeling that others paid and he did not. Once in a while his mother would put a dollar or two in an envelope and ask him to deliver it to the Sister Superior, on account. This was even more hateful. He always refused violently. August, however, didn't mind delivering the rare envelopes; indeed, he looked forward to the opportunity. He hated August for it, for making an issue of their poverty, for his willingness to remind the nuns that they were poor people. He had never wanted to go to Sister School anyway. The only thing that made it tolerable was baseball. When Sister Celia told him his mother had a beautiful soul, he knew she meant his mother was brave to sacrifice and deny for those little envelopes. But there was no bravery in it to him. It was awful, it was hateful, it made him and his brothers different from the others. Why, he did not know for certain—but it was there, a feeling that made them different to all the others in his eyes. It was somehow a part of the pattern that included his freckles, his need for a haircut, the patch on his knee, and being an Italian.

"Does your father go to Mass on Sunday, Arturo?"

"Sure," he said.

It choked in his throat. Why did he have to lie? His father only went to Mass on Christmas morning, and sometimes on Easter Sunday. Lie or not, it pleased him that his father scorned the Mass. He did not know why, but it pleased him. He remembered that argument of his father's. Svevo had said, if God is everywhere, why do I have to go to Church on Sunday? Why can't I go down to the Imperial Poolhall? Isn't God down there, too? His mother always shuddered in horror at this piece of theology, but he remembered how feeble her reply to it, the same reply he had learned in his catechism, and one his mother had learned out of the same catechism years before. It was our duty as Christians, the Catechism said. As for himself, sometimes he went to Mass and sometimes not. Those times he did not go, a great fear clutched him, and he was miserable and frightened until he had got it off his chest in the Confessional.

At four thirty, Sister Celia finished correcting her papers. He sat there wearily, exhausted and bruised by his own impatience to do something, anything. The room was almost dark. The moon had staggered out of the dreary eastern sky, and it was going to be a white moon if it ever got free. The room saddened him in the half light. It was a room for nuns to walk in, on quiet thick shoes. The empty desks spoke sadly of the children who had gone, and his own desk seemed to sympathize, its warm intimacy telling him to go home that it might be alone with the others. Scratched and marked with his initials, blurred and spotted with ink, the desk was as tired of him as he was of the desk. Now they almost hated one another, yet each so patient with the other.

Sister Celia stood up, gathering her papers.

"At five you may leave," she said. "But on one condition—"

His lethargy consumed any curiosity as to what that condition might be. Sprawled out with his feet twined around the desk in front of him, he could do no more than stew in his own disgust.

"I want you to leave here at five and go to the Blessed Sacrament, and I want you to ask the Virgin Mary to bless your mother and bring her all the happiness she deserves—the poor thing."

Then she left. The poor thing. His mother—the poor thing. It worked a despair in him that made his eyes fill up. Everywhere it was the same, always his mother—the poor thing, always poor and poor, always that, that word, always in him and around him, and suddenly he let go in that half darkened room and wept, sobbing the poor out of him, crying and choking, not for that, not for her, for his mother, but for Svevo Bandini, for his father, that look of his father's, those gnarled hands of his father's, for his father's mason tools, for the walls his father had built, the steps, the cornices, the ashpits and the cathedrals, and they were all so very beautiful, for that feeling in him when his father sang of Italy, of an Italian sky, of a Neapolitan bay.

At a quarter to five his misery had spent itself. The room was almost completely dark. He pulled his sleeve across his nose and felt a contentment rising in his heart, a good feeling, a restfulness that made the next fifteen minutes a mere nothing. He wanted to turn on the lights, but Rosa's house was beyond the empty lot across the street, and the school windows were visible from her back porch. She might see the light burning, and that would remind her that he was still in the classroom.

Rosa, his girl. She hated him, but she was his girl. Did she know that he loved her? Was that why she hated him? Could she see the mysterious things that went on inside him, and was that why she laughed at him? He crossed to the window and saw the light in the kitchen of Rosa's house. Somewhere under that light Rosa walked and breathed. Perhaps she was studying her lessons now, for Rosa was very studious and got the best grades in class.

Turning from the window, he moved to her desk. It was like no other in that room: it was cleaner, more girlish, the surface brighter and more varnished. He sat in her seat and the sensation thrilled him. His hands groped over the wood, inside the little shelf where she kept her books. His fingers found a pencil. He examined it closely: it was faintly marked with the imprint of Rosa's teeth. He kissed it. He kissed the books he found there, all of them so neatly bound with clean-smelling white oilcloth.

At five o'clock, his senses reeling with love and Rosa, Rosa, Rosa pouring from his lips, he walked down the stairs and into the winter evening. St. Catherine's Church was directly next to the school. Rosa, I love you!

In a trance he walked down the gloom shrouded middle aisle, the holy water still cold on the tips of his fingers and forehead, his feet echoing in the choir, the smell of incense, the smell of a thousand funerals and a thousand baptisms, the sweet odor of death and the tart odor of the living mingled in his nostrils, the hushed gasp of burning candles, the echo of himself walking on tiptoe down and down the long aisle, and in his heart, Rosa.

He knelt before the Blessed Sacrament and tried to pray as he had been told, but his mind shimmered and floated with the reverie of her name, and all at once he realized he was committing a sin, a great and horrible sin there in the presence of the Blessed Sacrament, for he was thinking of Rosa evilly, thinking of her in a way that the Catechism forbade. He squeezed his eyes tightly and tried to blot out the evil, but it returned stronger, and now his mind turned over the scene of unparalleled sinfulness, something he had never thought of before in his whole life, and he was gasping not only at the horror of his soul in the sight of God, but at the startling ecstasy of that new thought. He could not bear it. He might die for this: God might strike him dead instantly. He got up, blessed himself, and fled, running out of the Church, terrified, the sinful thought coming after him as if on wings. Even as he reached the freezing street, he wondered that he had ever made it alive, for the flight down that long aisle over which so many dead had been wheeled seemed endless. There was no trace of the evil thought in his mind once he reached the street and saw the evening's first stars. It was too cold for that. In a moment he was shivering, for though he wore three sweaters he possessed no mackinaw or gloves, and he slapped his hands to keep them warm. It was a block out of his way, but he wanted to pass Rosa's house. The Pinelli bungalow nestled beneath cottonwoods, thirty yards from the sidewalk. The blinds over the two front windows were down. Standing in the front path with his arms crossed and his hands squeezed under his armpits to keep them warm, he watched for a sign of Rosa, her silhouette as she crossed the line of vision through the window. He stamped his feet, his breath spouting white clouds. No Rosa. Then in the deep snow off the path his cold face bent to study the small foot-print of a girl. Rosa's—who's else but Rosa, in this yard. His cold fingers grubbed the snow from around the print, and with both hands he scooped it up and carried it away with him down the street . . .

He got home to find his two brothers eating dinner in the kitchen. Eggs again. His lips contorted as he stood over the stove, warming his hands. August's mouth was gorged with bread as he spoke.

"I got the wood, Arturo. You got to get the coal."

"Where's Mamma?"

"In bed," Federico said. "Grandma Donna's coming."

"Papa drunk yet?"

"He ain't home."

"Why does Grandma keep coming?" Federico said. "Papa always gets drunk."

"Ah, the old bitch!" Arturo said.

Federico loved swear words. He laughed. "The old bitchy bitch," he said.

"That's a sin," August said. "It's two sins."

Arturo sneered. "Whaddya' mean, *two* sins?"

"One for using a bad word, the other for not honoring thy father and mother."

"Grandma Donna's no mother of mine."

"She's your grandmother."

"Screw her."

"That's a sin too."

"Aw, shut your trap."

When his hands tingled, he seized the big bucket and the little bucket behind the stove and kicked open the back door. Swinging the buckets gingerly, he walked down the accurately cut path to the coal shed. The supply of coal was running low. It meant his mother would catch hell from Bandini, who never understood why so much coal was burned. The Big 4 Coal Company had, he knew, refused his father any more credit. He filled the buckets and marveled at his father's ingenuity at getting things without money. No wonder his father got drunk. He would get drunk too if he had to keep buying things without money.

The sound of coal striking the tin buckets roused Maria's hens in the coop across the path. They staggered sleepily into the moon sodden yard and gaped hungrily at the boy as he stooped in the doorway of the shed. They clucked their greeting, their absurd heads pushed through the holes in the chicken wire. He heard them, and standing up he watched them hatefully.

"Eggs," he said. "Eggs for breakfast, eggs for dinner, eggs for supper."

He found a lump of coal the size of his fist, stood back and measured his distance. The old brown hen nearest him got the blow in the neck as the whizzing lump all but tore her head loose and caromed off the chicken shed. She staggered, fell, rose weakly and fell again as the others screamed their fear and disappeared into the shed. The old brown hen was on her feet again, dancing giddily into the snow-covered section of the yard, a zig-zag of brilliant red painting weird patterns in the snow. She died slowly, dragging her bleeding head after her in a drift of snow that ascended toward the top of the fence. He watched the bird suffer with cold satisfaction. When it shuddered for the last time, he grunted and carried the buckets of coal to the kitchen. A moment later he returned and picked up the dead hen.

"What'd you do *that* for ?" August said. "It's a sin."

"Aw, shut your mouth," he said, raising his fist.

3.

MARIA WAS SICK. FEDERICO AND AUGUST TIP-
toed into the dark bedroom where she lay, so cold with
Winter, so warm with the fragrance of things on the dresser, the thin odor of Mamma's hair coming through, the
strong odor of Bandini, of his clothes somewhere in the
room. Maria opened her eyes. Federico was about to sob.
August looked annoyed.

"We're hungry," he said. "Where does it hurt?"

"I'll get up," she said.

They heard the crack of her joints, saw the blood seep
back into the white side of her face, sensed the staleness
of her lips and the misery of her being. August hated it.
Suddenly his own breath had that stale taste.

"Where does it hurt, Mamma?"

Federico said: "Why the heck does Grandma Donna
have to come to our house?"

She sat up, nausea crawling over her. She clinched her teeth to check a sudden retch. She had always been ill, but hers was ever sickness without symptom, pain without blood or bruise. The room reeled with her dismay. Together the brothers felt a desire to flee into the kitchen, where it was bright and warm. They left guiltily.

Arturo sat with his feet in the oven, supported on blocks of wood. The dead chicken lay in the corner, a trickle of red slipping from her beak. When Maria entered she saw it without surprise. Arturo watched Federico and August, who watched their mother. They were disappointed that the dead chicken had not annoyed her.

"Everybody has to take a bath right after supper," she said. "Grandma's coming tomorrow."

The brothers set up a groaning and wailing. There was no bathtub. Bathing meant pails of water into a wash tub on the kitchen floor, an increasingly hateful task to Arturo, since he was growing now and could no longer sit in the tub with any freedom.

For more than fourteen years Svevo Bandini had reiterated his promise to install a bath tub. Maria could remember the first day she walked into that house with him. When he showed her what he flatteringly termed the bathroom, he had quickly added that next week he would have a bath tub installed. After fourteen years he was still affirming it that way.

"Next week," he would say, "I'll see about that bath tub."

The promise had become family folklore. The boys enjoyed it. Year after year Federico or Arturo asked, "Papa, when we gonna have a bath tub?" and Bandini would answer in profound determination, "Next week," or, "The first of the week."

When they laughed to hear him say it over and over again, he glared at them, demanded silence and shouted, "What the hell's so funny?" Even he, when he bathed, grumbled and cursed the wash tub in the kitchen. The boys could hear him deprecating his lot with life, and his violent avowals.

"Next week, by God, next week!"

While Maria dressed the chicken for dinner, Federico shouted: "I get the leg!" and disappeared behind the stove with a pocket knife. Squatting on the kindling wood box, he carved boats to sail as he took his bath. He carved and stacked them, a dozen boats, big and small, enough wood indeed to fill the tub by half, to say nothing of water displacement by his own body. But the more the better: he could have a sea-battle, even if he did have to sit on some of his craft.

August was hunched in the corner studying the Latin liturgy of the Altar Boy at Mass. Father Andrew had given him the prayer-book as a reward for outstanding piety during the Holy Sacrifice, such piety being a triumph of sheer physical endurance, for whereas Arturo, who was also an Altar Boy, was always lifting his weight from one knee to the other as he knelt through the long services of High Mass, or scratching himself, or yawning, or forgetting to respond to the priest's words, August was never guilty of such impiety. Indeed, August was very proud of a more or less unofficial record he now held in the Altar Boy Society. To wit: He could kneel up straight with his hands reverently folded for a longer period of time than any other acolyte. The other Altar Boys freely acknowledged August's supremacy in this field, and not one of the forty members of the organization saw any sense in challenging him. That his talent as an endurance-kneeler went unchallenged often annoyed the champion.

August's great show of piety, his masterful efficiency as an Altar Boy, was a matter of everlasting satisfaction to Maria. Whenever the nuns or members of the parish mentioned August's ritualistic proclivities, it made her glow happily. She never missed a Sunday Mass at which August served. Kneeling in the first pew, at the foot of the main altar, the sight of her second son in his cassock and surplice lifted her to fulfillment. The flow of his robes as he walked, the precision of his service, the silence of his feet on lush red carpet, was reverie and dream, paradise on earth. Some day August would be a priest; all else became meaningless; she could suffer and slave; she could die and die again, but her womb had given God a priest, sanctifying her, a chosen one, mother of a priest, kindred of the Blessed Virgin. . . .

With Bandini it was different. August was very pious and desired to become a priest—*si*. But *Chi copro!* What the hell, he would get over that. The spectacle of his sons as Altar Boys gave him more amusement than spiritual satisfaction. The rare times he went to Mass and saw them, usually Christmas morning when the tremendous ceremony of Catholicism reached its most elaborate expression, it was not without chuckling that he watched his three sons in the solemn procession down the center aisle. Then he saw them not as consecrated children cloaked in expensive lace and deeply in communion with the Almighty; rather, such habiliments served to heighten the contrast, and he saw them simply and more vividly, as they really were, not only his sons but also the other boys—savages, irreverent kids uncomfortable and itching in their heavy cassocks. The sight of Arturo, choking with a tight celluloid collar against his ears, his freckled face red and bloated, his withering hatred of the whole ceremony made Bandini titter aloud. As for little Federico, he was the same, a devil for all his trappings. The seraphic sighs of women to the contrary notwithstanding, Bandini knew the embarrassment, the discomfort, the awful annoyance of the boys.

August wanted to be a priest; oh, he would get over that. He would grow up and forget all about it. He would grow up and be a man, or he, Svevo Bandini, would knock his goddamn block off.

Maria picked up the dead chicken by the legs. The boys held their noses and fled from the kitchen when she opened and dressed it.

"I get the leg," Federico said.

"We heard you the first time," Arturo said.

He was in a black mood, his conscience shouting questions about the murdered hen. Had he committed a mortal sin, or was the killing of the hen only a venial sin? Lying on the floor in the living room, the heat of the pot-bellied stove scorching one side of his body, he reflected darkly upon the three elements which, according to the Catechism, constituted a mortal sin. 1st, grievous matter; 2nd, sufficient reflection; 3rd full consent of the will.

His mind spiralled in gloomy productions. He recalled that story of Sister Justinus about the murderer who, all of his waking and sleeping hours, saw before his eyes the contorted face of the man he had murdered; the apparition taunting him, accusing him, until the murderer had gone in terror to confession and poured out his black crime to God.

Was it possible that he too would suffer like that? That happy, unsuspecting chicken. An hour ago the bird was alive, at peace with the earth. Now she was dead, killed in cold blood by his own hand. Would his life be haunted to the end by the face of a chicken? He stared at the wall, blinked his eyes, and gasped. It was there—the dead chicken was staring him in the face, clucking fiendishly! He leaped to his feet, hurried to the bedroom, locked the door:

"Oh Virgin Mary, give me a break! I didn't mean it! I swear to God I don't know why I done it! Oh please, dear chicken! Dear chicken, I'm sorry I killed you!"

He launched into a fusillade of Hail Marys and Our Fathers until his knees ached, until having kept accurate record of each prayer, he concluded that forty-five Hail Marys and nineteen Our Fathers were enough for true contrition. But a superstition about the number nineteen forced him to whisper one more Our Father that it might come out an even twenty. Then, his mind still fretting about possible stinginess he heaped on two more Hail Marys and two more Our Fathers just to prove beyond a doubt that he was not superstitious and had no faith in numbers, for the Catechism emphatically denounced any species of superstition whatever.

He might have prayed on, except that his mother called him to dinner. In the center of the kitchen table she had placed a plate piled high with brown fried chicken. Federico squealed and hammered his dish with a fork. The pious August bent his head and whispered grace before meals. Long after he had said the prayer he kept his aching neck bent, wondering why his mother made no comment. Federico nudged Arturo, then thumbed his nose at the devout August. Maria faced the stove. She turned around, the gravy pitcher in her hand, and saw August, his golden head so reverently tipped.

"Good boy, August," she smiled. "Good boy. God bless you!"

August raised his head and blessed himself. But by that time Federico had already raided the chicken dish and both legs were gone. One of them Federico gnawed; the other he had hidden between his legs. August's eyes searched the table in annoyance. He suspected Arturo, who sat with zestless appetite. Then Maria seated herself. In silence she spread margarine over a slice of bread.

Arturo's lips were locked in a grimace as he stared at the crisp, dismembered chicken. An hour ago that chicken had been happy, unaware of the murder that would befall it. He glanced at Federico, whose mouth dripped as he tore into the luscious flesh. It nauseated Arturo. Maria pushed the plate toward him.

"Arturo—you're not eating."

The tip of his fork searched with insincere perspicacity. He found a lonely piece, a miserable piece that looked even worse when he lifted it to his own plate—the gizzard. God, please don't let me be unkind to animals any more. He nibbled cautiously. Not bad. It had a delicious taste. He took another bite. He grinned. He reached for more. He ate with gusto, rummaging for white meat. He remembered where Federico had hidden that other leg. His hand slipped under the table and he filched it without anyone noticing the act, took it from Federico's lap. When he had finished the leg, he laughed and tossed the bone into his little brother's plate. Federico stared at it, pawing his lap in alarm:

"Damn you," he said. "Damn you, Arturo. You crook."

August looked at his little brother reproachfully, shaking his yellow head. Damn was a sinful word; possibly not a mortal sin; probably only a venial sin, but a sin for all that. He was very sad about it and was so glad he didn't use cuss words like his brothers.

It was not a large chicken. They cleaned the plate in the center of the table, and when only bones lay before them Arturo and Federico gnawed them open and sucked the marrow.

"Good thing Papa ain't coming home," Federico said. "We'd have to save some for him."

Maria smiled at them, gravy plastered over their faces, crumbs of chicken even in Federico's hair. She brushed them aside and warned about bad manners in front of Grandma Donna.

"If you eat the way you did tonight, she won't give you a Christmas present."

A futile threat. Christmas presents from Grandma Donna! Arturo grunted. "All she ever gives us is pajamas. Who the heck wants pajamas?"

"Betcha' Papa's drunk by now," Federico said. "Him and Rocco Saccone."

Maria's fist went white and tight. "That beast," she said. "Don't mention him at this table!"

Arturo understood his mother's hatred for Rocco. Maria was so afraid of him, so revolted when he came near. Her hatred of his life-long friendship with Bandini was tireless. They had been boys together in Abruzzi. In the early days before her marriage they had known women together, and when Rocco came to the house, he and Svevo had a way of drinking and laughing together without speaking, of muttering provincial Italian dialect and then laughing uproariously, a violent language of grunts and memories, teeming with implication, yet meaningless and always of a world in which she had never belonged and could never belong. What Bandini had done before his marriage she pretended not to care, but this Rocco Saccone with his dirty laughter which Bandini enjoyed and shared was a secret out of the past that she longed to capture, to lay open once and for all, for she seemed to know that, once the secrets of those early days were revealed to her, the private language of Svevo Bandini and Rocco Saccone would become extinct forever.

With Bandini gone, the house was not the same. After supper the boys, stupid with food, lay on the floor in the living room, enjoying the friendly stove in the corner. Arturo fed it coal, and it wheezed and chuckled happily, laughing softly as they sprawled around it, their appetites sodden.

In the kitchen Maria washed the dishes, conscious of one less dish to put away, one less cup. When she returned them to the pantry, Bandini's heavy battered cup, larger and clumsier than the others, seemed to convey an injured pride that it had remained unused throughout the meal. In the drawer where she kept the cutlery Bandini's knife, his favorite, the sharpest and most vicious table knife in the set, glistened in the light.

The house lost its identity now. A loose shingle whispered caustically to the wind; the electric light wires rubbed the gabled back porch, sneering. The world of inanimate things found voice, conversed with the old house, and the house chattered with cronish delight of the discontent within its walls. The boards under her feet squealed their miserable pleasure.

Bandini would not be home tonight.

The realization that he would not come home, the knowledge that he was probably drunk somewhere in the town, deliberately staying away, was terrifying. All that was hideous and destructive upon the earth seemed privy to the information. Already she sensed the forces of blackness and terror gathering around her, creeping in macabre formation upon the house.

Once the supper dishes were out of the way, the sink cleaned, the floor swept, her day abruptly died. Now nothing remained to occupy her. She had done so much sewing and patching over fourteen years under yellow light that her eyes resisted violently whenever she attempted it; headaches seized her, and she had to give it up until the day-time.

Sometimes she opened the pages of a woman's magazine whenever one came her way; those sleek bright magazines that shrieked of an American paradise for women: beautiful furniture, beautiful gowns: of fair women who found romance in yeast: of smart women discussing toilet paper. These magazines, these pictures represented that vague category: 'American women.' Always she spoke in awe of what 'the American women' were doing.

She believed those pictures. By the hour she could sit in the old rocker beside the window in the living room, ever turning the pages of a woman's magazine, methodically licking the tip of her finger and turning the page. She came away drugged with the conviction of her separation from that world of 'American women.'

Here was a side of her Bandini bitterly derided. He, for example, was a pure Italian, of peasant stock that went back deeply into the generations. Yet he, now that he had citizenship papers, never regarded himself as an Italian. No, he was an American; sometimes sentiment buzzed in his head and he liked to yell his pride of heritage; but for all sensible purposes he was an American, and when Maria spoke to him of what 'the American women' were doing and wearing, when she mentioned the activity of a neighbor, 'that American woman down the street,' it infuriated him. For he was highly sensitive to the distinction of class and race, to the suffering it entailed, and he was bitterly against it.

He was a bricklayer, and to him there was not a more sacred calling upon the face of the earth. You could be a king; you could be a conqueror, but no matter what you were you had to have a house; and if you had any sense at all it would be a brickhouse; and, of course, built by a union man, on the union scale. That was important.

But Maria, lost in the fairyland of a woman's magazine, gazing with sighs at electric irons and vacuum cleaners and automatic washing machines and electric ranges, had but to close the pages of that land of fantasy and look about her: the hard chairs, the worn carpets, the cold rooms. She had but to turn her hand and examine the palm, calloused from a washboard, to realize that she was not, after all, an American woman. Nothing about her, neither her complexion, nor her hands, nor her feet; neither the food she ate nor the teeth that chewed it—nothing about her, nothing, gave her kinship with 'the American women.'

She had no need in her heart for either book or magazine. She had her own way of escape, her own passage into contentment: her rosary. That string of white beads, the tiny links worn in a dozen places and held together by strands of white thread which in turn broke regularly, was, bead for bead, her quiet flight out of the world. Hail Mary, full of grace, the Lord is with thee. And Maria began to climb. Bead for bead, life and living fell away. Hail Mary, Hail Mary. Dream without sleep encompassed her. Passion without flesh lulled her. Love without death crooned the melody of belief. She was away: she was free; she was no longer Maria, American or Italian, poor or rich, with or without electric washing machines and vacuum cleaners; here was the land of all-possessing. Hail Mary, Hail Mary, over and over, a thousand and a hundred thousand times, prayer upon prayer, the sleep of the body, the escape of the mind, the death of memory, the slipping away of pain, the deep silent reverie of belief. Hail Mary and Hail Mary. It was for this that she lived.

Tonight the beaded passage into escape, the sense of joy the rosary brought her, was in her mind long before she turned out the kitchen light and walked into the living room, where her grunting, groggy sons were sprawled over the floor. The meal had been too much for Federico. Already he was heavily asleep. He lay with his face turned aside, his mouth wide open. August, flat on his stomach, stared blankly into Federico's mouth and reflected that, after he was ordained a priest, he would certainly get a rich parish and have chicken dinner every night.

Maria sank into the rocking chair by the window. The familiar crack of her knees caused Arturo to flinch in annoyance. She drew the beads from the pocket of her apron. Her dark eyes closed and the tired lips moved, a whispering audible and intense.

Arturo rolled over and studied his mother's face. His mind worked fast. Should he interrupt her and ask her for a dime for the movies, or should he save time and trouble by going into the bedroom and stealing it? There was no danger of being caught. Once his mother began her rosary she never opened her eyes. Federico was asleep, and as for August, he was too dumb and holy to know what was going on in the world anyway. He stood up and stretched himself.

"Ho hum. Guess I'll get me a book."

In the chilling darkness of his mother's bedroom he lifted the mattress at the foot of the bed. His fingers pawed the meager coins in the ragged purse, pennies and nickels, but so far no dimes. Then they closed around the familiar thin smallness of a ten cent piece. He returned the purse to its place within the coil spring and listened for suspicious sounds. Then with a flourish of noisy footsteps and loud whistling he walked into his own room and seized the first book his hand touched on the dresser.

He returned to the living room and dropped on the floor beside August and Federico. Disgust pulled at his face when he saw the book. It was the life of St. Teresa of the Little Flower of Jesus. He read the first line of the first page. 'I will spend my heaven doing good on Earth.' He closed the book and pushed it toward August.

"Fooey," he said. "I don't feel like reading. Guess I'll go out and see if any of the kids are on the hill coasting."

Maria's eyes remained closed, but she turned her lips faintly to denote that she had heard and approved of his plan. Then her head shook slowly from side to side. That was her way of telling him not to stay out late.

"I won't," he said.

Warm and eager under his tight sweaters, he sometimes ran, sometimes walked down Walnut Street, past the railroad tracks to Twelfth, where he cut through the filling station property on the corner, crossed the bridge, ran at a dead sprint through the park because the dark shadows of cottonwood scared him, and in less than ten minutes he was panting under the marquee of the Isis Theatre. As always in front of small town theatres, a crowd of boys his own age loafed about, penniless, meekly waiting the benevolence of the head usher who might, or might not, depending upon his mood, let them in free after the second show of the night was well under way. Often he too had stood out there, but tonight he had a dime, and with a good-natured smile for the hangers-on, he bought a ticket and swaggered inside.

He spurned the military usher who wagged a finger at him, and found his own way through the blackness. First he selected a seat in the very last row. Five minutes later he moved down two rows. A moment later he moved again. Little by little, two and three rows at a time, he edged his way toward the bright screen, until at last he was in the very first row and could go no farther. There he sat, his throat tight, his Adam's apple protruding as he squinted almost straight into the ceiling as Gloria Borden and Robert Powell performed in "Love On The River."

At once he was under the spell of that celluloid drug. He was positive that his own face bore a striking resemblance to that of Robert Powell, and he was equally sure that the face of Gloria Borden bore an amazing resemblance to his wonderful Rosa: thus he found himself perfectly at home, laughing uproariously at Robert Powell's witty comments, and shuddering with voluptuous delight whenever Gloria Borden looked passionate. Gradually Robert Powell lost his identity and became Arturo Bandini, and gradually Gloria Borden metamorphosed into Rosa Pinelli. After the big airplane crackup, with Rosa lying on the operating table, and none other than Arturo Bandini performing a precarious operation to save her life, the boy in the front seat broke into a sweat. Poor Rosa! The tears streamed down his face and he wiped his drooling nose with an impatient pull of his sweater sleeve across his face.

But he knew, he had a feeling all along, that young Doctor Arturo Bandini would achieve a medical miracle, and sure enough, it happened! Before he knew it, the handsome doctor was kissing Rosa; it was Springtime and the world was beautiful. Suddenly, without a word of warning, the picture was over, and Arturo Bandini, sniffling and crying, sat in the front row of the Isis theatre, horribly embarrassed and utterly disgusted with his chicken-hearted sentiment. Everybody in the Isis was staring at him. He was sure of it, since he bore so striking a resemblance to Robert Powell.

The effects of the drugged enchantment left him slowly. Now that the lights were on and reality returned, he looked about. No one sat within ten rows of him. He looked over his shoulder at the mass of pasty, bloodless faces in the center and rear of the theatre. He felt a streak of electricity in his stomach. He caught his breath in ecstatic fright. Out of that small sea of drabness, one countenance sparkled diamond-like, the eyes ablaze with beauty. It was the face of Rosa! And only a moment ago he had saved her on the operating table! But it was all such a miserable lie. He was here, the sole occupant of ten rows of seats. Lowering himself until the top of his head almost disappeared, he felt like a thief, a criminal, as he stole one more glance at that dazzling face. Rosa Pinelli! She sat between her mother and father, two extremely fat, double-chinned Italians, far toward the rear of the theatre. She could not see him; he was sure she was too far away to recognize him, yet his own eyes leaped the distance between them and he saw her miscroscopically, saw the loose curls peeking from under her bonnet, the dark beads around her neck, the starry sparkle of her teeth. So she had seen the picture too! Those black and laughing eyes of Rosa, they had seen it all. Was it possible that she had noticed the resemblance between himself and Robert Powell?

But no: there really wasn't any resemblance at all; not really. It was just a movie, and he was down front, and he felt hot and perspiring beneath his sweaters. He was afraid to touch his hair, afraid to lift his hand up there and smooth back his hair. He knew it grew upward and unkempt like weeds. People were always recognizing him because his hair was never combed and he always needed a haircut. Perhaps Rosa had already discovered him. Ah—why hadn't he combed his hair down? Why was he always forgetting things like that? Deeper and deeper he sank into the seat, his eyes rolling backward to see if his hair showed over the chair-back. Cautiously, inch by inch, he lifted his hand to smooth down his hair. But he couldn't make it. He was afraid she might see his hand.

When the lights went out again, he was panting with relief. But as the second show began, he realized he would have to leave. A vague shame strangled him, a consciousness of his old sweaters, of his clothes, a memory of Rosa laughing at him, a fear that, unless he slipped away now, he might meet her in the foyer as she left the theatre with her parents. He could not bear the thought of confronting them. Their eyes would look upon him; the eyes of Rosa would dance with laughter. Rosa knew all about him; every thought and deed. Rosa knew that he had stolen a dime from his mother, who needed it. She would look at him, and she would know. He had to beat it; or had to get out of there; something might happen; the lights might go on again and she would see him; there might be a fire; anything might happen; he simply had to get up and get out of there. He could be in a classroom with Rosa, or on the schoolgrounds; but this was the Isis Theatre, and he looked like a lousy bum in these lousy clothes, different from everybody else, and he had stolen the money: he had no right to be there. If Rosa saw him she could read in his face that he had stolen the money. Only a dime, only a venial sin, but it was a sin any way you looked at it. He arose and took long, quick, silent steps up the aisle, his face turned aside, his hand shielding his nose and eyes. When he reached the street the huge cold of the night leaped as though with whips upon him, and he started to run, the wind in his face stinging him, flecking him with fresh, new thoughts.

As he turned into the walk that led to the porch of his home, the sight of his mother silhouetted in the window released the tension of his soul; he felt his skin breaking like a wave, and in a rush of feeling he was crying, the guilt pouring from him, inundating him, washing him away. He opened the door and found himself in his home, in the warmth of his home, and it felt deep and wonderful. His brothers had gone to bed, but Maria had not moved, and he knew her eyes had not opened, her fingers ever moving with blind conviction around the endless circle of beads. Oh boy, she looked swell, his mother, she looked keen. Oh kill me God because I'm a dirty dog and she's a beauty and I ought to die. Oh Mamma, look at me because I stole a dime and you keep on praying. Oh Mamma kill me with your hands.

He fell on his knees and clung to her in fright and joy and guilt. The rocker jerked to his sobs, the beads rattling in her hands. She opened her eyes and smiled down at him, her thin fingers gently raking his hair, telling herself he needed a haircut. His sobs pleased her like caresses, gave her a sense of tenderness toward her beads, a feeling of unity of beads and sobs.

"Mamma," he groped. "I did something."

"It's alright," she said. "I knew."

That surprised him. How could she have possibly known? He had swiped that dime with consummate perfection. He had fooled her, and August, and everyone. He had fooled them all.

"You were saying the rosary, and I didn't want to bother you," he lied. "I didn't want to interrupt you right in the middle of the rosary."

She smiled. "How much did you take?"

"A dime. I coulda' taken all of it, but I only took a dime."

"I know."

That annoyed him. "But *how* do you know? Did you see me take it?"

"The water's hot in the tank," she said. "Go take your bath."

He arose and began to pull off his sweaters.

"But how did you know? Did you look? Did you peek? I thought you always closed your eyes when you said the rosary."

"Why shouldn't I know?" she smiled. "You're always taking dimes out of my pocketbook. You're the only one who ever does. I know it every time. Why, I can tell by the sound of your feet!"

He untied his shoes and kicked them off. His mother was a pretty darned smart woman after all. But what if next time he should take off his shoes and slip into the bedroom barefoot ? He was giving the plan deep consideration as he walked naked into the kitchen for his bath.

He was disgusted to find the kitchen floor soaked and cold. His two brothers had raised havoc with the room. Their clothes were scattered about, and one wash tub was full of greyish soapy water and pieces of water-soaked wood : Federico's battleships.

It was too darn cold for a bath that night. He decided to fake it. Filling a wash tub, he locked the kitchen door, produced a copy of *Scarlet Crime,* and settled down to reading *Murder For Nothing* as he sat naked upon the warm oven door, his feet and ankles thawing in the wash tub. After he had read for what he thought was the normal length of time it took really to have a bath, he hid *Scarlet Crime* on the back porch, cautiously wet his hair with the palm of one hand, rubbed his dry body with a towel until it glowed a savage pink, and ran shivering to the living room. Maria watched him crouch near the stove as he rubbed the towel into his hair, grumbling all the while of his detestation of taking baths in the dead of winter. As he strode off to bed, he was pleased with himself at such a masterful piece of deception. Maria smiled to. Around his neck as he disappeared for the night, she saw a ring of dirt that stood out like a black collar. But she said nothing. The night was indeed too cold for bathing.

Alone now, she turned out the lights and continued with her prayers. Occasionally through the reverie she listened to the house. The stove sobbed and moaned for fuel. In the street a man smoking a pipe walked by. She watched him, knowing he could not see her in the darkness. She compared him with Bandini; he was taller, but he had none of Svevo's gusto in his step. From the bedroom came the voice of Federico, talking in his sleep. Then Arturo, mumbling sleepily: "Aw, shut up!" Another man passed in the street. He was fat, the steam pouring from his mouth and into the cold air. Svevo was a much finer looking man than he; thank God Svevo was not fat. But these were distractions. It was sacrilegious to allow stray thoughts to interfere with prayer. She closed her eyes tightly and made a mental checklist of items for the Blessed Virgin's consideration.

She prayed for Svevo Bandini, prayed that he would not get too drunk and fall into the hands of the police, as he had done on one occasion before their marriage. She prayed that he would stay away from Rocco Saccone, and that Rocco Saccone would stay away from him. She prayed for the quickening of time, that the snow might melt and Spring hurry to Colorado, that Svevo could go back to work again. She prayed for a happy Christmas and for money. She prayed for Arturo, that he would stop stealing dimes, and for August, that he might become a priest, and for Federico, that he might be a good boy. She prayed for clothes for them all, for money for the grocer, for the souls of the dead, for the souls of the living, for the world, for the sick and the dying, for the poor and the rich, for courage, for strength to carry on, for forgiveness in the error of her ways.

She prayed a long, fervent prayer that the visit of Donna Toscana would be a short one, that it would not bring too much misery all around, and that some day Svevo Bandini and her mother might enjoy a peaceful relationship. That last prayer was almost hopeless, and she knew it. How even the mother of Christ could arrange a cessation of hostilities between Svevo Bandini and Donna Toscana was a problem that only Heaven could solve. It always embarrassed her to bring this matter to the Blessed Virgin's attention. It was like asking for the moon on a silver brooch. After all, the Virgin Mother had already interceded to the extent of a splendid husband, three fine children, a good home, lasting health, and faith in God's mercy. But peace between Svevo and his mother-in-law, well, there were requests that taxed even the generosity of the Almighty and the Blessed Virgin Mary.

Donna Toscana arrived at noon Sunday. Maria and the children were in the kitchen. The agonized moan of the porch beneath her weight told them it was Grandma. An iciness settled in Maria's throat. Without knocking, Donna opened the door and poked her head inside. She spoke only Italian.

"Is he here—the Abruzzian dog?"

Maria hurried from the kitchen and threw her arms around her mother. Donna Toscana was now a huge woman, always dressed in black since the death of her husband. Beneath the outer black silk were petticoats, four of them, all brightly colored. Her bloated ankles looked like goiters. Her tiny shoes seemed ready to burst beneath the pressure of her two hundred and fifty pounds. Not two but a dozen breasts seemed crushed into her bosom. She was constructed like a pyramid, without hips. There was so much flesh in her arms that they hung not downward but at an angle, her puffed fingers dangling like sausages. She had virtually no neck at all. When she turned her head the drooping flesh moved with the melancholy of melting wax. A pink scalp showed beneath her thin white hair. Her nose was thin and exquisite, but her eyes were like trampled concord grapes. Whenever she spoke her false teeth chattered obliviously a language all their own.

Maria took her coat and Donna stood in the middle of the room, smelling it, the fat crinkling in her neck as she conveyed to her daughter and grandsons the impression that the odor in her nostrils was definitely a nasty one, a very filthy one. The boys sniffed suspiciously. Suddenly the house *did* possess an odor they had never noticed before. August thought about his kidney trouble two years before, wondering if, after two years, the odor of it was still in existence.

"Hi ya, Grandma," Federico said.

"Your teeth look black," she said. "Did you wash them this morning?"

Federico's smile vanished and the back of his hand covered his lips as he lowered his eyes. He tightened his mouth and resolved to slip into the bathroom and look in the mirror as soon as he could. Funny how his teeth *did* taste black.

Grandma kept sniffing.

"What *is* this malevolent odor?" she asked. "Surely your father is not at home."

The boys understood Italian, for Bandini and Maria often used it.

"No, Grandma," Arturo said. "He isn't home."

Donna Toscana reached into the folds of her breasts and drew out her purse. She opened it and produced a ten cent piece at the tips of her fingers, holding it out.

"Now," she smiled. "Who of my three grandsons is the most honest? To the one who is, I will give this *deci soldi*. Tell me quickly: is your father drunk?"

"Ah, *mamma mio*," Maria said. "Why do you ask that?"

Without looking at her, Grandma answered, "Be still, woman. This is a game for the children."

The boys consulted one another with their eyes: They were silent, anxious to betray their father but not anxious enough. Grandma was so stingy, yet they knew her purse was filled with dimes, each coin the reward for a piece of information about Papa. Should they let this question pass and wait for another—one not quite so unfavorable to Papa —or should one of them answer before the other? It was not a question of answering truthfully: even if Papa *wasn't* drunk. The only way to get the dime was in answering to suit Grandma.

Maria stood by helplessly. Donna Toscana wielded a tongue like a serpent, ever ready to strike out in the presence of the children: half-forgotten episodes from Maria's childhood and youth, things Maria preferred that her boys not know lest the information encroach upon her dignity: little things the boys might use against her. Donna Toscana had used them before. The boys knew that their Mamma was stupid in school, for Grandma had told them. They knew that Mamma had played house with Nigger children and got a licking for it. That Mamma had vomited in the choir of St. Dominic's at a hot high mass. That Mamma, like August, had wet the bed, but, unlike August, had been forced to wash out her own nighties. That Mamma had run away from home and the police had brought her back (not *really* run away, only strayed away, but Grandma insisted she had run away). And they knew other things about

Mamma. She refused to work as a little girl and had been locked in the cellar by the hour. She never was and never would be a good cook. She screamed like a hyena when her children were born. She was a fool or she would never have married a scoundrel like Svevo Bandini . . . . and she had no self-respect, otherwise why did she always dress in rags? They knew that Mamma was a weakling, dominated by her dog of a husband. That Mamma was a coward who should have sent Svevo Bandini to jail a long time ago. So it was better not to antagonize her mother. Better to remember the Fourth Commandment, to be respectful toward her mother so that her own children by example would be respectful toward her.

"Well," Grandma repeated. "Is he drunk?"

A long silence.

Then Federico: "Maybe he is, Grandma. We don't know."

"Mamma mio," Maria said. "Svevo is not drunk. He is away on business. He will be back any minute now."

"Listen to your mother," Donna said. "Even when she was old enough to know better she never flushed the toilet. And now she tries to tell me your vagabond father is not drunk! But he *is drunk!* Is he not, Arturo? Quick—for *deci soldi!*"

"I dunno, Grandma. Honest."

"Bah!" she snorted. "Stupid children of a stupid parent!"

She threw a few coins at their feet. They pounced upon them like savages, fighting and tumbling over the floor.

Maria watched the squirming mass of arms and legs. Donna Toscana's head shook miserably.

"And you smile," she said. "Like animals they claw themselves to pieces, and their mother smiles her approval. Ah, poor America! Ah, America, thy children shall tear out one another's throats and die like blood-thirsty beasts!"

"But *Mamma mio,* they are boys. They do no harm."

"Ah, poor America!" Donna said. "Poor, hopeless America!"

She began her inspection of the house. Maria had prepared for this: carpets and floors swept, furniture dusted, the stoves polished. But a dust rag will not remove stains from a leaking ceiling; a broom will not sweep away the worn places on a carpet; soap and water will not disturb the omnipresence of the marks of children: the dark stains around door knobs, here and there a grease spot that was born suddenly; a child's name crudely articulate; random designs of tic-tac-toe games that always ended without a winner; toe marks at the bottom of doors, calendar pictures that sprouted mustaches over night; a shoe that Maria had put away in the closet not ten minutes before; a sock; a towel; a slice of bread and jam in the rocking chair.

For hours Maria had worked and warned—and this was her reward. Donna Toscana walked from room to room, her face a crust of dismay. She saw the boys' room: the bed carefully made, a blue spread smelling of moth balls neatly completing it; she noticed the freshly ironed curtains, the shining mirror over the dresser, the rag rug at the bedside so precisely in order, everything so monastically impersonal, and under the chair in the corner—a pair of Arturo's dirty shorts, kicked there, and sprawled out like the section of a boy's body sawed in half.

The old woman raised her hands and wailed.

"No hope," she said. "Ah, woman! Ah, America!"

"Well, how did *that* get there?" Maria said. "The boys are always so careful."

She picked up the garment and hastily shoved it under her apron, Donna Toscana's cold eyes upon her for a full minute after the pair of shorts had disappeared.

"Blighted woman. Blighted, defenseless woman."

All afternoon it was the same, Donna Toscana's relentless cynicism wearing her down. The boys had fled with their dimes to the candy store. When they did not return after an hour Donna lamented the weakness of Maria's authority. When they did return, Federico's face smeared with chocolate, she wailed again. After they had been back an hour, she complained that they were too noisy, so Maria sent them outside. After they were gone she prophesied that they would probably die of influenza out there in the snow. Maria made her tea. Donna clucked her tongue and concluded that it was too weak. Patiently Maria watched the clock on the stove. In two hours, at seven o'clock, her mother would leave. The time halted and limped and crawled in agony.

"You look bad," Donna said. "What has happened to the color in your face?"

With one hand Maria smoothed her hair.

"I feel fine," she said. "All of us are well."

"Where is he?" Donna said. "That vagabond."

"Svevo is working, *Mamma mio*. He is figuring a new job."

"On Sunday?" she sneered. "How do you know he is not out with some *puttana?*"

"Why do you say such things? Svevo is not that kind of a man."

"The man you married is a brutal animal. But he married a stupid woman, and so I suppose he will never be exposed. Ah, America! Only in this corrupt land could such things happen."

While Maria prepared dinner she sat with her elbows on the table, her chin in her hands. The fare was to be spaghetti and meat balls. She made Maria scour the spaghetti kettle with soap and water. She ordered the long box of spaghetti brought to her, and she examined it carefully for evidences of mice. There was no ice-box in the house, the meat being kept in a cupboard on the back porch. It was round steak, ground for meat balls.

"Bring it here," Donna said.

Maria placed it before her. She tasted it with the tip of her finger. "I thought so," she frowned. "It is spoiled."

"But that is impossible!" Maria said. "Only last night I bought it."

"A butcher will always cheat a fool," she said.

Dinner was delayed a half hour because Donna insisted that Maria wash and dry the already clean plates. The kids came in, ravenously hungry. She ordered them to wash their hands and faces, to put on clean shirts and wear neckties. They growled and Arturo muttered "The old bitch," as he fastened a hated necktie. By the time all was ready the dinner was cold. The boys ate it anyhow. The old woman ate listlessly, a few strands of spaghetti before her. Even these displeased her, and she pushed her plate away.

"The dinner is badly prepared," she said. "This spaghetti tastes like dung."

Federico laughed.

"It's good, though."

"Can I get you something else, *Mamma mio?*"

"No!"

After dinner she sent Arturo to the filling station to phone for a cab. Then she left, arguing with the cab driver, trying to bargain the fare to the depot from twenty-five to twenty cents. After she was gone Arturo stuffed a pillow into his shirt, wound an apron around it, and waddled around the house, sniffing contemptuously. But no one laughed. No one cared.

4.

NO BANDINI, NO MONEY, NO FOOD. IF BANDINI
were home, he would say, "Charge it."

Monday afternoon, and still no Bandini, and that grocery
bill! She could never forget it. Like a tireless ghost it filled
the winter days with dread.

Next door to the Bandini house was Mr. Craik's grocery
store. In the early years of his marriage Bandini had opened
a credit business with Mr. Craik. At first he managed to
keep the bills paid. But as the children grew older and
hungrier, as bad year followed bad year, the grocery bill
whizzed into crazy figures. Every year since his marriage
things got worse for Svevo Bandini. Money! After fifteen
years of marriage Bandini had so many bills that even
Federico knew he had no intention or opportunity to pay
them.

But the grocery bill harassed him. Owing Mr. Craik a

hundred dollars, he paid fifty—if he had it. Owing two hundred, he paid seventy-five—if he had it. So it was with all the debts of Svevo Bandini. There was no mystery about them. There were no hidden motives, no desire to cheat in their non-payment. No budget could solve them. No planned economy could alter them. It was very simple: the Bandini family used up more money than he earned. He knew his only escape lay in a streak of good luck. His tireless presumption that such good luck was coming forestalled his complete desertion and kept him from blowing out his brains. He constantly threatened both, but did neither. Maria did not know how to threaten. It was not in her nature.

But Mr. Craik the grocer complained unceasingly. He never quite trusted Bandini. If the Bandini family had not lived next door to his store, where he could keep his eye on it, and if he had not felt that ultimately he would receive at least most of the money owed him, he would not have allowed further credit. He sympathized with Maria and pitied her with that cold pity small businessmen show to the poor as a class, and with that frigid self-defensive apathy toward individual members of it. Christ, he had bills to pay too.

Now that the Bandini account was so high—and it rose by leaps throughout each Winter—he abused Maria, even insulted her. He knew that she herself was honest to the point of childish innocence, but that did not seem relevant when she came to the store to increase the account. Just like she owned the place! He was there to sell groceries, not give them away. He dealt in merchandise, not feelings. Money was owed him. He was allowing her additional credit. His demands for money were in vain. The only thing to do was keep after her until he got it. Under the circumstances, his attitude was the best he could possibly muster.

Maria had to coax herself to a pitch of inspired audacity in order to face him each day. Bandini paid no attention to her mortification at the hands of Mr. Craik.

Charge it, Mr. Craik. Charge it.

All afternoon and until an hour before dinner Maria walked the house, waiting for that desperate inspiration so necessary for a trip to the store. She went to the window and sat with hands in her apron pockets, one fist around her rosary—waiting. She had done it before, only two days ago, Saturday, and the day before that, all the days before that, Spring, Summer, Winter, year in, year out. But now her courage slept from overuse and would not rise. She couldn't go to that store again, face that man.

From the window, through the pale Winter evening, she saw Arturo across the street with a gang of neighborhood kids. They were involved in a snowball fight in the empty lot. She opened the door.

"Arturo!"

She called him because he was the oldest. He saw her

· 97 ·

standing in the doorway. It was a white darkness. Deep shadows crept fast across the milky snow. The street lamps burned coldly, a cold glow in a colder haze. An automobile passed, its tire chains clanging dismally.

"Arturo!"

He knew what she wanted. In disgust he clinched his teeth. He *knew* she wanted him to go to the store. She was a yellow-belly, just plain yellow, passing the buck to him, afraid of Craik. Her voice had that peculiar tremor that came with grocery-store time. He tried to get out of it by pretending that he hadn't heard, but she kept calling until he was ready to scream and the rest of the kids, hypnotized by that tremor in her voice, stopped throwing snowballs and looked at him, as though begging him to do something.

He tossed one more snowball, watched it splatter, and then trudged through the snow and across the icy pavement. Now he could see her plainly. Her jaws quivered from the twilight cold. She stood with arms squeezing her thin body, tapping her toes to keep them warm.

"Whaddya' want?" he said.

"It's cold," she said. "Come inside, and I'll tell you."

"What *is* it, Ma? I'm in a hurry."

"I want you to go to the store."

"The store? No! I know why you want me to go—because you're afraid on account of the bill. Well, I ain't going. Never."

"Please go," she said. "You're big enough to understand. You know how Mr. Craik is."

Of course he knew. He hated Craik, that skunk, always asking him if his father was drunk or sober, and what did his father *do* with his money, and how do you Wops live without a cent, and how does it happen that your old man never stays home at night, what's he got—a woman on the side, eating up his money? He knew Mr. Craik and he hated him.

"Why can't August go?" he said. "Heck sakes, I do all the work around here. Who gets the coal and wood? I do. Every time. Make August go."

"But August won't go. He's afraid."

"Blah. The coward. What's there to be afraid of? Well, I'm not going."

He turned and tramped back to the boys. The snowball fight was resumed. On the opposition side was Bobby Craik, the grocer's son. I'll get you, you dog. On the porch Maria called again. Arturo did not answer. He shouted so that her voice might be drowned out. Now it was darkness, and Mr. Craik's windows bloomed in the night. Arturo kicked a stone from the frozen earth and shaped it within a snowball. The Craik boy was fifty feet away, behind a tree. He threw with a frenzy that strained his whole body, but it missed—sailing a foot out of line.

Mr. Craik was whacking a bone with his cleaver on the chopping block when Maria entered. As the door squealed he looked up and saw her—a small insignificant figure in an old black coat with a high fur collar, most of the fur shed so that white hide spots appeared in the dark mass. A weary brown hat covered her forehead—the face of a very old little child hiding beneath it. The faded gloss from her rayon stockings made them a yellowish tan, accentuating the small bones and white skin beneath them, and making her old shoes seem even more damp and ancient. She walked like a child, fearfully, on tiptoe, awed, to that familiar place from which she invariably made her purchases, farthest away from Mr. Craik's chopping block, where the counter met the wall.

In the earlier years she used to greet him. But now she felt that perhaps he would not relish such familiarity, and she stood quietly in her corner, waiting until he was ready to wait on her.

Seeing who it was, he paid no attention, and she tried to be an interested and smiling spectator as he swung his cleaver. He was of middle height, partially bald, wearing celluloid glasses—a man of forty-five. A thick pencil rested behind one ear, and a cigarette behind the other. His white apron hung to his shoe tops, a blue butcher string wound many times around his waist. He was hacking a bone inside a red and juicy rump.

She said: "It looks good, doesn't it?"

He flipped the steak over and over, swished a square of paper from the roll, spread it over the scales, and tossed the steak upon it. His quick, soft fingers wrapped it expertly. She estimated that it was close to two dollars worth, and she wondered who had purchased it—possibly one of Mr. Craik's rich American women customers up on University Hill.

Mr. Craik heaved the rest of the rump upon his shoulder and disappeared inside the ice-box, closing the door behind him. It seemed he stayed a long time in that ice-box. Then he emerged, acted surprised to see her, cleared his throat, clicked the ice-box door shut, padlocked it for the night, and disappeared into the back room.

She supposed he was going to the wash room to wash his hands, and that made her wonder if she was out of Gold Dust Cleanser, and then, all at once, everything she needed for the house crashed through her memory, and a weakness like fainting overcame her as quantities of soap, margarine, meat, potatoes, and so many other things seemed to bury her in an avalanche.

Craik reappeared with a broom and began to sweep the sawdust around the chopping block. She lifted her eyes to the clock: ten minutes to six. Poor Mr. Craik! He looked tired. He was like all men, probably starved for a hot meal.

Mr. Craik finished his sweeping and paused to light a

cigarette. Svevo smoked only cigars, but almost all American men smoked cigarettes. Mr. Craik looked at her, exhaled, and went on sweeping.

She said, "It is cold weather we're having."

But he coughed, and she supposed he hadn't heard, for he disappeared into the back room and returned with a dust pan and a paper box. Sighing as he bent down, he swept the sawdust into the pan and poured it into the paper box.

"I don't like this cold weather," she said. "We are waiting for Spring, especially Svevo."

He coughed again, and before she knew it he was carrying the box back to the rear of the store. She heard the splash of running water. He returned, drying his hands on his apron, that nice white apron. At the cash register, very loudly, he rang up NO SALE. She changed her position, moving her weight from one foot to the other. The big clock ticked away. One of those electric clocks with the strange ticks. Now it was exactly six o'clock.

Mr. Craik scooped the coins from the cash box and spread them on the counter. He tore a slip of paper from the roll and reached for his pencil. Then he leaned over and counted the day's receipts. Was it possible that he was not aware of her presence in the store? Surely he had seen her come in and stand there! He wet the pencil on the tip of his pink tongue and began adding up the figures. She raised her eyebrows and strolled to the front window to look at the fruits and vegetables. Oranges: sixty cents a dozen. Asparagus fifteen cents a pound. Oh my, oh my. Apples two pounds for a quarter.

"Strawberries!" she said. "And in Winter, too! Are they California strawberries, Mr. Craik?"

He swept the coins into a bank sack and went to the safe, where he squatted and fingered the combination lock. The big clock ticked. It was ten minutes after six when he closed the safe. Immediately he disappeared into the rear of the store again.

Now she no longer faced him. Shamed, exhausted, her feet had tired, and with hands clasped in her lap she sat on an empty box and stared at the frosted front windows. Mr. Craik took off his apron and threw it over the chopping block. He lifted the cigarette from his lips, dropped it to the floor and crushed it deliberately. Then he went to the back room again, returning with his coat. As he straightened his collar, he spoke to her for the first time.

"Come on, Mrs. Bandini. My God, I can't hang around here all night long."

At the sound of his voice she lost her balance. She smiled to conceal her embarrassment, but her face was purplish and her eyes lowered. Her hands fluttered at her throat.

"Oh!" she said. "I was—waiting for you!"

"What'll it be, Mrs. Bandini—shoulder steak?"

She stood in the corner and pursed her lips. Her heart

beat so fast she could think of nothing at all to say now. She said: "I think I want—"

"Hurry up, Mrs. Bandini. My God, you been here about a half hour now, and you ain't made up your mind yet."

"I thought—"

"Do you want shoulder steak?"

"How much is shoulder steak, Mr. Craik?"

"Same price. My God, Mrs. Bandini. You been buying it for years. Same price. Same price all the time."

"I'll take fifty cents worth."

"Why didn't you tell me before?" he said. "Here I went and put all that meat in the ice-box."

"Oh, I'm sorry, Mr. Craik."

"I'll get it this time. But after this, Mrs. Bandini, if you want my business, come early. My God, I got to get home sometime tonight."

He brought out a cut of shoulder and stood sharpening his knife.

"Say," he said. "What's Svevo doing these days?"

In the fifteen odd years that Bandini and Mr. Craik knew one another, the grocer always referred to him by his first name. Maria always felt that Craik was afraid of her husband. It was a belief that secretly made her very proud. Now they talked of Bandini, and she told him again the monotonous tale of a bricklayer's misfortunes on the Colorado winters.

"I seen Svevo last night," Craik said. "Seen him up around Effie Hildegarde's house. Know her ?"

No—she didn't know her.

"Better watch that Svevo," he said with insinuating humor. "Better keep your eye on him. Effie Hildegarde's got lots of money."

"She's a widow too," Craik said, studying the meat scale, "Own's the street car company."

Maria watched his face closely. He wrapped and tied the meat, slapped it before her on the counter. "Owns lots of real estate in this town too. Fine looking woman, Mrs. Bandini."

Real estate ? Maria sighed with relief.

"Oh, Svevo knows lots of real estate people. He's probably figuring some job for her."

She was biting her thumbnail when Craik spoke again.

"What else, Mrs. Bandini ?"

She ordered the rest: flour, potatoes, soap, margarine, sugar. "I almost forgot !" she said. "I want some fruit too, a half dozen of those apples. The children like fruit."

Mr. Craik swore under his breath as he whipped a sack open and dropped apples into it. He did not approve of fruit for the Bandini account: he could see no reason for poor people indulging in luxury. Meat and flour—yes. But why should they eat fruit when they owed him so much money ?

"Good God," he said. "This charging business has got to

stop, Mrs. Bandini! I tell you it can't go on like this. I ain't had a penny on that bill since September."

"I'll tell him!" she said, retreating. "I'll tell him, Mr. Craik."

"Ack! A lot of good that does!"

She gathered her packages.

"I'll tell him, Mr. Craik! I'll tell him tonight."

Such a relief to step into the street! How tired she was. Her body ached. Yet she smiled as she breathed the cold night air, hugging her packages lovingly, as though they were life itself.

Mr. Craik was mistaken. Svevo Bandini was a family man. And why shouldn't he talk to a woman who owned real estate?

5.

ARTURO BANDINI WAS PRETTY SURE THAT HE
wouldn't go to hell when he died. The way to hell was the
committing of mortal sin. He had committed many, he believed, but the Confessional had saved him. He always got
to Confession on time—that is, before he died. And he
knocked on wood whenever he thought of it—he always
would get there on time—before he died. So Arturo was
pretty sure he wouldn't go to hell when he died. For two
reasons. The Confessional, and the fact that he was a fast
runner.

But Purgatory, that midway place between Hell and
Heaven, disturbed him. In explicit terms the Catechism
stated the requirements for Heaven: a soul had to be absolutely clean, without the slightest blemish of sin. If the
soul at death was not clean enough for Heaven, and not
befouled enough for Hell, there remained that middle re-

gion, that Purgatory where the soul burned and burned until it was purged of its blemishes.

In Purgatory there was one consolation: soon or late you were a cinch for Heaven. But when Arturo realized that his stay in Purgatory might be seventy million trillion billion years, burning and burning and burning, there was little consolation in ultimate Heaven. After all, a hundred years was a long time. And a hundred and fifty million years was incredible.

No: Arturo was sure he would never go straight to Heaven. Much as he dreaded the prospect, he knew that he was in for a long session in Purgatory. But wasn't there something a man could do to lessen the Purgatory ordeal of fire? In his Catechism he found the answer to this problem.

The way to shorten the awful period in Purgatory, the Catechism stated, was by good works, by prayer, by fasting and abstinence, and by piling up indulgences. Good works were out, as far as he was concerned. He had never visited the sick, because he knew no such people. He had never clothed the naked because he had never seen any naked people. He had never buried the dead because they had undertakers for that. He had never given alms to the poor because he had none to give; besides, 'alms' always sounded to him like a loaf of bread, and where could he get loaves of bread? He had never harbored the injured because—well, he didn't know—it sounded like something people did on seacoast towns, going out and rescuing sailors injured in shipwrecks. He had never instructed the ignorant because after all, he was ignorant himself, otherwise he wouldn't be forced to go to this lousy school. He had never enlightened the darkness because that was a tough one he never did understand. He had never comforted the afflicted because it sounded dangerous and he knew none of them anyway: most cases of measles and smallpox had quarantine signs on the doors.

As for the ten commandments he broke practically all of them, and yet he was sure that not all of these infringements were mortal sins. Sometimes he carried a rabbit's foot, which was superstition, and therefore a sin against the first commandment. But was it a mortal sin? That always bothered him. A mortal sin was a serious offense. A venial sin was a slight offense. Sometimes, playing baseball, he crossed bats with a fellow-player: this was supposed to be a sure way to get a two base hit. And yet he knew it was superstition. Was it a sin? And was it a mortal sin or a venial sin? One Sunday he had deliberately missed mass to listen to the broadcast of the world series, and particularly to hear of his god, Jimmy Foxx of the Athletics. Walking home after the game it suddenly occurred to him that he had broken the first commandment: thou shalt not have strange gods before me. Well, he had committed a mortal sin in missing mass, but was it another mortal sin to prefer Jimmy Foxx to God Almighty during the world series ? He had gone to Confession, and there the matter grew more complicated. Father Andrew had said, "If you think it's a mortal sin, my son, then it is a mortal sin." Well, heck. At first he had thought it was only a venial sin, but he had to admit that, after considering the offense for three days before Confession, it had indeed become a mortal sin.

The third commandment. It was no use even thinking about that, for Arturo said 'God damn it' on an average of four times a day. Nor was that counting the variations : God damn this and God damn that. And so, going to Confession each week, he was forced to make wide generalizations after a futile examination of his conscience for accuracy. The best he could do was confess to the priest, "I took the name of the Lord in vain about sixty-eight or seventy times." Sixty-eight mortal sins in one week, from the second commandment alone. Wow ! Sometimes, kneeling in the cold church awaiting Confessional, he listened in alarm to the beat of his heart, wondering if it would stop and he drop dead before he got those things off his chest. It exasperated him, that wild beating of his heart. It compelled him not to run but often to walk, and very slowly, to Confessional, lest he overdo the organ and drop in the street.

"Honor thy father and thy mother." Of course he honored his father and his mother ! Of course. But there was a catch in it : the Catechism went on to say that any disobedience of thy father and thy mother was dishonor. Once more he was out of luck. For though he did indeed honor his mother and father, he was rarely obedient. Venial sins? Mortal sins? The classifications pestered him. The number of sins against that commandment exhausted him; he would count them to the hundreds as he examined his days hour by hour. Finally he came to the conclusion that they were only venial sins, not serious enough to merit Hell. Even so, he was very careful not to analyze this conclusion too deeply.

He had never killed a man, and for a long time he was sure that he would never sin against the fifth commandment. But one day the class in Catechism took up the study of the fifth commandment, and he discovered to his disgust that it was practically impossible to avoid sins against it. Killing a man was not the only thing: the by-products of the commandment included cruelty, injury, fighting, and all forms of viciousness to man, bird, beast, and insect alike.

Goodnight, what was the use? He enjoyed killing blue-bottle flies. He got a big kick out of killing muskrats, and birds. He loved to fight. He hated those chickens. He had had a lot of dogs in his life, and he had been severe and often harsh with them. And what of the prairie dogs he had killed, the pigeons, the pheasants, the jackrabbits? Well, the only thing to do was to make the best of it. Worse, it was a sin to even think of killing or injuring a human being. That sealed his doom. No matter how he tried, he could not resist expressing the wish of violent death against some people: like Sister Mary Corta, and Craik the grocer, and the freshmen at the university, who beat the kids off with clubs and forbade them to sneak into the big games at the stadium. He realized that, if he wasn't actually a murderer, he was the equivalent in the eyes of God.

One sin against that fifth commandment that always seethed in his conscience was an incident the summer before, when he and Paulie Hood, another Catholic boy, had captured a rat alive and crucified it to a small cross with tacks, and mounted it on an anthill. It was a ghastly and horrible thing that he never forgot. But the awful part of it was, they had done this evil thing on Good Friday, and right after saying the Stations of the Cross! He had confessed that sin shamefully, weeping as he told it, with true contrition, but he knew it had piled up many years in Purgatory, and it was almost six months before he even dared kill another rat.

Thou shalt not commit adultery; thou shalt not think about Rosa Pinelli, Joan Crawford, Norma Shearer, and Clara Bow. Oh gosh, oh Rosa, oh the sins, the sins, the sins. It began when he was four, no sin then because he was ignorant. It began when he sat in a hammock one day when he was four, rocking back and forth, and the next day he came back to the hammock between the plum tree and the apple tree in the back yard, rocking back and forth.

What did he know about adultery, evil thoughts, evil actions? Nothing. It was fun in the hammock. Then he learned to read, and the first of many things he read were the commandments. When he was eight he made his first Confession, and when he was nine he had to take the commandments apart and find out what they meant.

Adultery. They didn't talk about it in the fourth grade Catechism class. Sister Mary Anna skipped it and spent most of the time talking about Honor thy Father and Mother and Thou Shalt Not Steal. And so it was, for vague reasons he never could understand, that to him adultery always has had something to do with bank robbery. From his eighth year to his tenth, examining his conscience before Confession, he would pass over 'Thou shalt not commit adultery' because he had never robbed a bank.

The man who told him about adultery wasn't Father Andrew, and it wasn't one of the nuns, but Art Montgomery at the Standard Station on the corner of Arapahoe and Twelfth. From that day on his loins were a thousand angry hornets buzzing in a nest. The nuns never talked about adultery. They only talked about evil thoughts, evil words, evil actions. That Catechism! Every secret of his heart, every sly delight in his mind was already known to that Catechism. He could not beat it, no matter how cautiously he tiptoed through the pinpoints of its code. He couldn't go to the movies anymore because he only went to the movies to see the shapes of his heroines. He liked 'love' pictures. He liked following girls up the stairs. He liked girls' arms, legs, hands, feet, their shoes and stockings and dresses, their smell and their presence. After his twelfth year the only things in life that mattered were baseball and girls, only he called them women. He liked the sound of the word. Women, women, women. He said it over and over because it was a secret sensation. Even at Mass, when there were fifty or a hundred of them around him, he reveled in the secrecy of his delights.

And it was all a sin—the whole thing had the sticky sensation of evil. Even the sound of some words was a sin. Ripple. Supple. Nipple. All sins. Carnal. The flesh. Scarlet. Lips. All sins. When he said the Hail Mary. Hail Mary full of grace, the Lord is with thee and blessed art thou among women, and blessed is the fruit of thy womb. The word shook him like thunder. Fruit of thy womb. Another sin was born.

Every week he staggered into the church of a Saturday afternoon, weighted down by the sins of adultery. Fear drove him there, fear that he would die and then live on forever in eternal torture. He did not dare lie to his confessor. Fear tore his sins out by the roots. He would confess it all fast, gushing with his uncleanliness, trembling to be pure. I committed a bad action I mean two bad actions and I thought about a girl's legs and about touching her in a bad place and I went to the show and thought bad things and I was walking along and a girl was getting out of a car and it was bad and I listened to a bad joke and laughed and a bunch of us kids were watching a couple of dogs and I said something bad, it was my fault, they didn't say anything, I did, I did it all, I made them laugh with a bad idea and I tore a picture out of a magazine and she was naked and I knew it was bad but did it anyway. I thought a bad thing about Sister Mary Agnes; it was bad and I kept on thinking. I also thought bad things about some girls who were laying on the grass and one of them had her dress up high and I kept on looking and knowing it was bad. But I'm sorry. It was my fault, all my fault, and I'm sorry, sorry.

He would leave the Confessional, and say his penance, his teeth gritted, his fist tightened, his neck rigid, vowing with body and soul to be clean forevermore. A sweetness would at last pervade him, a soothing lull him, a breeze cool him, a loveliness caress him. He would walk out of the church in a dream, and in a dream he would walk, and if no one was looking he'd kiss a tree, eat a blade of grass, blow kisses at the sky, touch the cold stones of the church wall with fingers of magic, the peace in his heart like nothing save a chocolate malted, a three-base hit, a shining window to be broken, the hypnosis of that moment that comes before sleep.

No, he wouldn't go to Hell when he died. He was a fast runner, always getting to Confession on time. But Purgatory awaited him. Not for him the direct, pure route to eternal bliss. He would get there the hard way, by detour. That was one reason why Arturo was an Altar Boy. Some piety on this earth was bound to lessen the Purgatory period.

He was an Altar Boy for two other reasons. In the first place, despite his ceaseless howls of protests, his mother insisted on it. In the second place, every Christmas season the girls in the Holy Name Society feted the Altar Boys with a banquet.

Rosa, I love you.

She was in the auditorium with the Holy Name Girls, decorating the tree for the Altar Boy Banquet. He watched from the door, feasting his eyes upon the triumph of her tiptoed loveliness. Rosa: tinfoil and chocolate bars, the smell of a new football, goal posts with bunting, a home run with the bases full. I am an Italian too, Rosa. Look, and my eyes are like yours. Rosa, I love you.

Sister Mary Ethelbert passed.

"Come, come, Arturo. Don't dawdle there."

She was in charge of the Altar Boys. He followed her black flowing robes to the 'little auditorium' where some seventy boys who comprised the male student body awaited her. She mounted the rostrum and clapped her hands for silence.

"All right boys, do take your places."

They lined up, thirty-five couples. The short boys were in front, the tall boys in the rear. Arturo's partner was Wally O'Brien, the kid who sold the Denver Posts in front of the First National Bank. They were twenty-fifth from the front, the tenth from the rear. Arturo detested this fact. For eight years he and Wally had been partners, ever since kindergarten. Each year found them moved back farther, and yet they had never made it, never grown tall enough to make it back to the last three rows where the big guys stood, where the wisecracks came from. Here it was, their last year in this lousy school, and they were still stymied around a bunch of sixth and seventh grade punks. They concealed their humiliation by an exceedingly tough and blasphemous exterior, shocking the sixth grade punks into a grudging and awful respect for their brutal sophistication.

But Wally O'Brien was lucky. He didn't have any kid brothers in the line to bother him. Each year, with increasing alarm, Arturo had watched his brothers August and Federico moving toward him from the front rows. Federico was now tenth from the front. Arturo was relieved to know that this youngest of his brothers would never pass him in the line-up. For next June, thank God, Arturo graduated, to be through forever as an Altar Boy.

But the real menace was the blonde head in front of him, his brother August. Already August suspected his impending triumph. Whenever the line was called to order he seemed to measure off Arturo's height with a contemptuous sneer. For indeed, August was the taller by an eighth of an inch, but Arturo, usually slouched over, always managed to straighten himself enough to pass Sister Mary Ethelbert's supervision. It was an exhausting process. He had to crane his neck and walk on the balls of his feet, his heels a half inch off the floor. Meanwhile he kept August in complete submission by administering smashing kicks with his knee whenever Sister Mary Ethelbert wasn't looking.

They did not wear vestments, for this was only practice. Sister Mary Ethelbert led them out of the little auditorium and down the hall, past the big auditorium, where Arturo caught a glance of Rosa sprinkling tinsel on the Christmas tree. He kicked August and sighed.

Rosa, me and you: a couple of Italians.

They marched down three flights of stairs and across the yard to the front doors of the church. The holy water fonts were frozen hard. In unison, they genuflected; Wally O'Brien's finger spearing the boy's in front of him. For two hours they practiced, mumbling Latin responses, genuflecting, marching in miltary piousness. *Ad deum qui loctificat, juventutem meum.*

At five o'clock, bored and exhausted, they were finished. Sister Mary Ethelbert lined them up for final inspection. Arturo's toes ached from bearing his full weight. In weariness he rested himself on his heels. It was a moment of carelessness for which he paid dearly. Sister Mary Ethelbert's keen eye just then observed a bend in the line, beginning and ending at the top of Arturo Bandini's head. He could read her thoughts, his weary toes rising in vain to the effort. Too late, too late. At her suggestion he and August changed places.

His new partner was a kid named Wilkins, fourth grader who wore celluloid glasses and picked his nose. Behind him, triumphantly sanctified, stood August, his lips sneering implacably, no word coming from him. Wally O'Brien looked at his erstwhile partner in crestfallen sadness, for Wally too had been humiliated by the intrusion of this upstart sixth grader. It was the end for Arturo. Out of the corner of his mouth he whispered to August.

"You dirty—" he said. "Wait'll I get you outside."

Arturo was waiting after practice. They met at the corner. August walked fast, as if he hadn't seen his brother. Arturo quickened his pace.

"What's your hurry, Tall Man?"

"I'm not hurrying, Shorty."

"Yes you are, Tall Man. And how would you like some snow rubbed in your face?"

"I wouldn't like it. And you leave me alone—Shorty."

"I'm not bothering you, Tall Man. I just want to walk home with you."

"Don't you try anything now."

"I wouldn't lay a hand on you, Tall Man. What makes you think I would?"

They approached the alley between the Methodist Church and the Colorado Hotel. Once beyond that alley, August was safe in the view of the loungers at the hotel window. He sprang forward to run, but Arturo's fist seized his sweater.

"What's the hurry, Tall Man?"

"If you touch me, I'll call a cop."

"Oh, I wouldn't do that."

A coupe passed, moving slowly. Arturo followed his brother's sudden open-mouthed stare at the occupants, a man and a woman. The woman was driving, and the man had his arm at her back.

"Look!"

But Arturo had seen. He felt like laughing. It was such a strange thing. Effie Hildegarde drove the car, and the man was Svevo Bandini.

The boys examined one another's faces. So that was why Mamma had asked all those questions about Effie Hildegarde! If Effie Hildegarde was good-looking. If Effie Hildegarde was a 'bad' woman.

Arturo's mouth softened to a laugh. The situation pleased him. That father of his! That Svevo Bandini! Oh boy— and Effie Hildegarde was a swell looking dame too!

"Did they see us?"

Arturo grinned. "No."

"Are you sure?"

"He had his arm around her, didn't he?"

August frowned.

"That's bad. That's going out with another woman. The ninth commandment."

They turned into the alley. It was a short cut. Darkness came fast. Water puddles at their feet were frozen in the growing darkness. They walked along, Arturo smiling. August was bitter.

"It's a sin. Mamma's a swell mother. It's a sin."

"Shut up."

They turned from the alley on Twelfth Street. The Christmas shopping crowd in the business district separated them now and then, but they stayed together, waiting as one another picked his way through the crowd. The street lamps went on.

"Poor Mamma. She's better than that Effie Hildegarde."

"Shut up."

"It's a sin."

"What do you know about it? Shut up."

"Just because Mamma hasn't got good clothes . . ."

"Shut up, August."

"It's a mortal sin."

"You're dumb. You're too little. You don't know anything."

"I know a sin. Mamma wouldn't do that."

The way his father's arm rested on her shoulder. He had seen her many times. She had charge of the girls' activities at the Fourth of July celebration in the Court House Park. He had seen her standing on the Court House steps the summer before, beckoning with her arms, calling the girls together for the big parade. He remembered her teeth, her pretty teeth, her red mouth, her fine plump body. He had left his friends to stand in the shadows and watch as she talked to the girls. Effie Hildegarde. Oh boy, his father was a wonder!

And he was like his father. A day would come when he and Rosa Pinelli would be doing it too. Rosa, let's get into the car and drive out in the country, Rosa. Me and you, out in the country Rosa. You drive the car and we'll kiss, but you drive, Rosa.

"I bet the whole town knows it," August said.

"Why shouldn't they? You're like everybody else. Just because Papa's poor, just because he's an Italian."

"It's a sin," he said, kicking viciously at frozen chunks of snow. "I don't care what he is—or how poor, either. It's a sin."

"You're dumb. A saphead. You don't savvy anything."

August did not answer him. They took the short path over the trestle bridge that spanned the creek. They walked in single file, heads down, careful of the limitations of the deep path through the snow. They took the trestle bridge on tiptoe, from railroad tie to tie, the frozen creek thirty feet below them. The quiet evening spoke to them, whispering of a man riding in a car somewhere in the same twilight, a woman not his own riding with him. They descended the crest of the railroad line and followed a faint trail which they themselves had made all that Winter in the comings and goings to and from school, through the Alzi pasture, with great sweeps of white on either side of the path, untouched for months, deep and glittering in the evening's birth. Home was a quarter of a mile away, only a block beyond the fences of the Alzi pasture. Here in this great pasture they had spent a great part of their lives. It stretched from the backyards of the very last row of houses in the town, weary frozen cottonwoods strangled in the death pose of long winters on one side, and a creek that no longer laughed on the other. Beneath that snow was white sand once very hot and excellent after swimming in the creek. Each tree held memories. Each fence post measured a dream, enclosing it for fulfillment with each new Spring. Beyond that pile of stones, between those two tall cottonwoods, was the graveyard of their dogs and Suzie, a cat who had hated the dogs but lay now beside them. Prince, killed by an automobile; Jerry, who ate the poison meat; Pancho the fighter, who crawled off and died after his last fight. Here they had killed snakes, shot birds, speared frogs, scalped Indians, robbed banks, completed wars, reveled in peace. But in that twilight their father rode with Effie Hildegarde, and the silent white sweep of the pasture land was only a place for walking on a strange road to home.

"I'm going to tell her," August said.

Arturo was ahead of him, three paces away. He turned around quickly. "You keep still," he said. "Mamma's got enough trouble."

"I'll tell her. She'll fix him."

"You shut up about this."

"It's against the ninth commandment. Mamma's our mother, and I'm going to tell."

Arturo spread his legs and blocked the path. August tried to step around him, the snow two feet deep on either side of the path. His head was down, his face set with disgust and pain. Arturo took both lapels of his mackinaw and held him.

"You keep still about this."

August shook himself loose.

"Why should I? He's our father, ain't he? Why does he have to do that?"

"Do you want Mamma to get sick?"

"Then what did he do it for?"

"Shut up! Answer my question. Do you want Mamma to be sick? She will if she hears about it."

"She won't get sick."

"I know she won't—because you're not telling."

"I am too."

The back of his hand caught August across the eyes."

"I said you're not going to tell !"

August's lips quivered like jelly.

"I'm telling."

Arturo's fist tightened under his nose.

"You see this ? You get it if you tell."

Why should August want to tell ? What if his father *was* with another woman ? What difference did it make, so long as his mother didn't know ? And besides, this wasn't another woman : this was Effie Hildegarde, one of the richest women in town. Pretty good for his father ; pretty swell. She wasn't as good as his mother—no : but that didn't have anything to do with it.

"Go ahead and hit me. I'm telling."

The hard fist pushed into August's cheek. August turned his head away contemptuously. "Go ahead. Hit me. I'm telling."

"Promise not to tell or I'll knock your face in."

"Pooh. Go ahead. I'm telling."

He tilted his chin forward, ready for any blow. It infuriated Arturo. Why did August have to be such a damn fool ? He didn't want to hit him. Sometimes he really enjoyed knocking August around, but not now. He opened his fist and clapped his hands on his hips in exasperation.

"But look, August," he argued. "Can't you see that it won't help to tell Mamma? Can't you just see her crying? And right now, at Christmas time too. It'll hurt her. It'll hurt her like hell. You don't want to hurt Mamma, you don't want to hurt your own mother, do you? You mean to tell me you'd go up to your own mother and say something that would hurt the hell out of her? Ain't that a sin, to do that?"

August's cold eyes blinked their conviction. The vapors of his breath flooded Arturo's face as he answered sharply. "But what about him? I suppose he isn't committing a sin. A worse sin than any I commit."

Arturo gritted his teeth. He pulled off his cap and threw it into the snow. He beseeched his brother with both fists. "God damn you! You're not telling."

"I am too."

With one blow he cut August down, a left to the side of his head. The boy staggered backward, lost his balance in the snow, and floundered on his back. Arturo was on him, the two buried in the fluffy snow beneath the hardened crust. His hands encircled August's throat. He squeezed hard.

"You gonna tell?"

The cold eyes were the same.

He lay motionless. Arturo had never known him that way before. What should he do? Hit him? Without relaxing his grip on August's neck he looked off toward the trees beneath which lay his dead dogs. He bit his lip and sought vainly within himself the anger that would make him strike.

Weakly he said, "Please, August. Don't tell."

"I'm telling."

So he swung. It seemed that the blood poured from his brother's nose almost instantly. It horrified him. He sat straddling August, his knees pinning down August's arms. He could not bear the sight of August's face. Beneath the mask of blood and snow August smiled defiantly, the red stream filling his smile.

Arturo knelt beside him. He was crying, sobbing with his head on August's chest, digging his hands into the snow and repeating: "Please August. Please! You can have anything I got. You can sleep on any side of the bed you want. You can have all my picture show money."

August was silent, smiling.

Again he was furious. Again he struck, smashing his fist blindly into the cold eyes. Instantly he regretted it, crawling in the snow around the quiet, limp figure.

Defeated at last, he rose to his feet. He brushed the snow from his clothes, pulled his cap down and sucked his hands to warm them. Still August lay there, blood still pouring from his nose: August the triumphant, stretched out like one dead, yet bleeding, buried in the snow, his cold eyes sparkling their serene victory.

Arturo was too tired. He no longer cared.

"Okay, August."

Still August lay there.

"Get up, August."

Without accepting Arturo's arm he crawled to his feet. He stood quietly in the snow, wiping his face with a handkerchief, fluffing the snow from his blonde hair. It was five minutes before the bleeding stopped. They said nothing. August touched his swollen face gently. Arturo watched him.

"You all right now?"

He did not answer as he stepped into the path and walked toward the row of houses. Arturo followed, shame silencing him: shame and hopelessness. In the moonlight he noticed that August limped. And yet it was not a limp so much as a caricature of one limping, like the pained embarrassed gait of the tenderfoot who had just finished his first ride on a horse. Arturo studied it closely. Where had he seen that before? It seemed so natural to August. Then he remembered: that was the way August used to walk out of the bedroom two years before, on those mornings after he had wet the bed.

"August," he said. "If you tell Mamma, I'll tell everybody that you pee the bed."

He had not expected more than a sneer, but to his surprise August turned around and looked him squarely in the face. It was a look of incredulity, a taint of doubt crossing the once cold eyes. Instantly Arturo sprang to the kill, his senses excited by the impending victory.

"Yes, sir!" he shouted. "I'll tell everybody. I'll tell the whole world. I'll tell every kid in the school. I'll write notes to every kid in the school. I'll tell everybody I see. I'll tell it and tell it to the whole town. I'll tell them August Bandini pees the bed. I'll tell 'em!"

"No!" August choked. "No, Arturo!"

He shouted at the top of his voice.

"Yes sir, all you people of Rocklin, Colorado! Listen to this: August Bandini pees the bed! He's twelve years old and he pees the bed. Did you ever hear of anything like that? Yipee! Everybody listen!"

"Please, Arturo! Don't yell. I won't tell. Honest I won't Arturo. I won't say a word! Only don't yell like that. I don't pee the bed, Arturo. I used to, but I don't now."

"Promise not to tell Mamma?"

August gulped as he crossed his heart and hoped to die.

"Okay," Arturo said. "Okay."

Arturo helped him to his feet and they walked home.

6.

NO QUESTION ABOUT IT: PAPA'S ABSENCE
had its advantages. If he were home the scrambled eggs for
dinner would have had onions in them. If he were home
they wouldn't have been permitted to gouge out the white
of the bread and eat only the crust. If he were home they
wouldn't have got so much sugar.

Even so, they missed him. Maria was so listless. All day
she swished in carpet slippers, walking slowly. Sometimes
they had to speak twice before she heard them. Afternoons
she sat drinking tea, staring into the cup. She let the dishes
go. One afternoon an incredible thing happened: a fly appeared. A fly! And in Winter! They watched it soaring
near the ceiling. It seemed to move with great difficulty, as
though its wings were frozen. Federico climbed a chair
and killed the fly with a rolled newspaper. It fell to the floor.
They got down on their knees and examined it. Federico

held it between his fingers. Maria knocked it from his hand.
She ordered him to the sink, and to use soap and water.
He refused. She seized him by the hair and dragged him to
his feet.

"You do what I tell you!"

They were astonished: Mamma had never touched them,
had never said an unkind thing to them. Now she was listless again, deep in the ennui of a tea cup. Federico washed
and dried his hands. Then he did a surprising thing. Arturo
and August were convinced that something was wrong,
for Federico bent over and kissed his mother in the depths
of her hair. She hardly noticed it. Absently she smiled.
Federico slipped to his knees and put his head in her lap.
Her fingers slid over the outlines of his nose and lips. But
they knew that she hardly noticed Federico. Without a
word she got up, and Federico looked after her in disappointment as she walked to the rocking chair by the window in the front room. There she remained, never moving,
her elbow on the window sill, her chin in her hand as she
watched the cold deserted street.

Strange times. The dishes remained unwashed. Sometimes they went to bed and the bed wasn't made. It didn't
matter but they thought about it, of her in the front room
by the window. Mornings she lay in bed and did not get up
to see them off to school. They dressed in alarm, peeking
at her from the bedroom door. She lay like one dead, the

rosary in her hand. In the kitchen the dishes had been washed sometime during the night. They were surprised again, and disappointed: for they had awakened to expect a dirty kitchen. It made a difference. They enjoyed the change from a clean to a dirty kitchen. But there it was, clean again, their breakfast in the oven. They looked in before leaving for school. Only her lips moved.

Strange times.

Arturo and August walked to school.

"Rember, August. Remember your promise."

"Huh. I don't have to tell. She knows it already."

"No, she doesn't."

"Then why does she act like that?"

"Because she thinks it. But she doesn't really know it."

"It's the same."

"No it isn't."

Strange times. Christmas coming, the town full of Christmas trees, and the Santa Claus men from the Salvation Army ringing bells. Only three more shopping days before Christmas. They stood with famine-stricken eyes before shop-windows. They sighed and walked on. They thought the same: it was going to be a lousy Christmas, and Arturo hated it, because he could forget he was poor if they didn't remind him of it: every Christmas was the same, always unhappy, always wanting things he never thought about and having them denied. Always lying to the kids: telling them he was going to get things he could never possibly own. The rich kids had their day at Christmas. They could spread it on, and he had to believe them.

Wintertime, the time for standing around radiators in the cloak rooms, just standing there and telling lies. Ah, for Spring! Ah, for the crack of the bat, the sting of a ball on soft palms! Wintertime, Christmas time, rich kid time: they had high top boots and bright mufflers and fur-lined gloves. But it didn't worry him very much. His time was the Springtime. No high top boots and fancy mufflers on the playing field! Can't get to first base because you got a classy necktie. But he lied with the rest of them. What was he getting for Christmas? Oh, a new watch, a new suit, a lot of shirts and ties, a new bicycle, and a dozen Spalding Official National League Baseballs.

But what of Rosa?

I love you, Rosa. She had a way about her. She was poor too, a coal miner's daughter, but they flocked around her and listened to her talk, and it didn't matter, and he envied her and was proud of her, wondering if those who listened ever considered that he was an Italian too, like Rosa Pinelli.

Speak to me, Rosa. Look this way just once, over here Rosa, where I am watching.

He had to get her a Christmas present, and he walked the streets and peered into windows and bought her jewels and gowns. You're welcome, Rosa. And here is a ring I bought you. Let me put it on your finger. There. Oh, it's nothing Rosa. I was walking along Pearl Street, and I came to Cherry's Jewelry Shop, and I went in and bought it. Expensive ? Naaaw. Three hundred, is all. I got plenty of money, Rosa. Haven't you heard about my father ? We're rich. My father's uncle in Italy. He left us everything. We come from fine people back there. We didn't know about it, but come to find out, we were second cousins of the Duke of Abruzzi. Distantly related to the King of Italy. It doesn't matter, though. I've always loved you, Rosa, and just because I come from royal blood never will make any difference.

Strange times. One night he got home earlier than usual. He found the house empty, the back door wide open. He called his mother but got no answer. Then he noticed that both stoves had gone out. He searched every room in the house. His mother's coat and hat were in the bedroom. Then where could she be ?

He walked into the back yard and called her.

"Ma ! Oh, Ma ! Where are you ?"

He returned to the house and built a fire in the front room. Where could she be without her hat and coat in this weather ? God damn his father ! He shook his fist at his father's hat hanging in the kitchen. God damn you, why don't you come home ! Look what you're doing to Mamma ! Darkness came suddenly and he was frightened. Somewhere in that cold house he could smell his mother, in every room, but she was not there. He went to the back door and yelled again.

"Ma! Oh, Ma! Where are you?"

The fire went out. There was no more coal or wood. He was glad. It gave him an excuse to leave the house and fetch more fuel. He seized a coal bucket and started down the path.

In the coal shed he found her, his mother, seated in the darkness in the corner, seated on a mortar board. He jumped when he saw her, it was so dark and her face so white, numb with cold, seated in her thin dress, staring at his face and not speaking, like a dead woman, his mother frozen in the corner. She sat away from the meager pile of coal in the part of the shed where Bandini kept his mason's tools, his cement and sacks of lime. He rubbed his eyes to free them from the blinding light of snow, the coal bucket dropped at his side as he squinted and watched her form gradually assume clarity, his mother sitting on a mortar board in the darkness of the coal shed. Was she crazy? And what was that she held in her hand?

"Mamma!" he demanded. "What're you *doing* in here?"

No answer, but her hand opened and he saw what it was: a trowel, a mason's trowel, his father's. The clamor and protest of his body and mind took hold of him. His mother in the darkness of the coal shed with his father's trowel. It was an intrusion upon the intimacy of a scene that belonged to him alone. His mother had no right in this place. It was as though she had discovered him there, committing a boy-sin, that place, identically where he had sat those times; and she was there, angering him with his memories and he hated it, she there, holding his father's trowel. What good did that do? Why did she have to go around reminding herself of him, fooling with his clothes, touching his chair? Oh, he had seen her plenty of times—looking at his empty place at the table; and now, here she was, holding his trowel in the coal shed, freezing to death and not caring, like a dead woman. In his anger he kicked the coal bucket and began to cry.

"Mamma!" he demanded. "What're you doing! Why are you out here? You'll die out here, Mamma! You'll freeze!"

She arose and staggered toward the door with white hands stretched ahead of her, the face stamped with cold, the blood gone from it as she walked past him and into the semi-darkness of the evening. How long she had been there he did not know, possibly an hour, possibly more, but he knew she must be half dead with cold. She walked in a daze, staring here and there as if she had never known that place before.

He filled the coal bucket. The shed smelled tartly of lime and cement. Over one rafter hung a pair of Bandini's over-alls. He grabbed at them and ripped the overalls in two. It was all right to go around with Effie Hildegarde, he liked that all right, but why should his mother suffer so much, making him suffer? He hated his mother too; she was a fool, killing herself on purpose, not caring about the rest of them, him and August and Federico. They were all fools. The only person with any sense in the whole family was himself.

Maria was in bed when he got back to the house. Fully clothed she lay shivering beneath the covers. He looked at her and made grimaces of impatience. Well, it was her own fault: why did she want to go out like that? Yet he felt he should be sympathetic.

"You all right, Mamma?"

"Leave me alone," her trembling mouth said. "Just leave me alone, Arturo."

"Want the hot water bottle?"

She did not reply. Her eyes glanced at him out of their corners, quickly, in exasperation. It was a look he took for hatred, as if she wanted him out of her sight forever, as though he had something to do with the whole thing. He whistled in surprise: gosh, his mother was a strange woman; she was taking this too seriously.

He left the bedroom on tiptoe, not afraid of her but of what his presence might do to her. After August and Federico got home, she arose and cooked dinner: poached eggs, toast, fried potatoes, and an apple apiece. She did not touch the food herself. After dinner they found her at the same place, the front window, staring at the white street, her rosary clicking against the rocker.

Strange times. It was an evening of only living and breathing. They sat around the stove and waited for something to happen. Federico crawled to her chair and placed his hand on her knee. Still in prayer, she shook her head like one hypnotized. It was her way of telling Federico not to interrupt her, or to touch her, to leave her alone.

The next morning she was her old self, tender and smiling through breakfast. The eggs had been prepared "Mamma's way," a special treat, the yolks filmed by the whites. And would you look at her! Hair combed tightly, her eyes big and bright. When Federico dumped his third spoonful of sugar into his coffee cup, she remonstrated with mock sternness.

"Not that way, Federico! Let me show you."

She emptied the cup into the sink.

"If you want a sweet cup of coffee, I'll give it to you." She placed the sugar bowl instead of the coffee cup on Federico's saucer. The bowl was half full of sugar. She filled it the rest of the way with coffee. Even August laughed, though he had to admit there might be a sin in it—wastefulness.

Federico tasted it suspiciously.

"Swell," he said. "Only there's no room for the cream."

She laughed, clutching her throat, and they were glad to see her happy, but she kept on laughing, pushing her chair

away and bending over with laughter. It wasn't that funny;
it couldn't be. They watched her miserably, her laughter
not ending even though their blank faces stared at her.
They saw her eyes fill with tears, her face swelling to purple.
She got up, one hand over her mouth, and staggered to the
sink. She drank a glass of water until it sputtered in her
throat and she could not go on, and finally she staggered
into the bedroom and lay on the bed, where she laughed.

Now she was quiet again.

They arose from the table and looked in at her on the
bed. She was rigid, her eyes like buttons in a doll, a funnel
of vapors pouring from her panting mouth and into the
cold air.

"You kids go to school," Arturo said. "I'm staying home."

After they were gone, he went to the bedside.

"Can I get you something, Ma?"

"Go away, Arturo. Leave me alone."

"Should I call Dr. Hastings?"

"No. Leave me alone. Go away. Go to school. You'll be
late."

"Should I try to find Papa?"

"Don't you dare."

Suddenly that seemed the right thing to do.

"I'm going to," he said. "That's just what I'm going to
do." He hurried for his coat.

"Arturo!"

She was out of bed like a cat. When he turned around in the clothes closet, one of his arms inside a sweater, he gasped to see her beside him so quickly. "Don't you go to your father! You hear me—don't you dare!" She bent so close to his face that hot spittle from her lips sprinkled it. He backed away to the corner and turned his back, afraid of her, afraid to even look at her. With strength that amazed him she took him by the shoulder and swung him around.

"You've seen him, haven't you? He's with that woman."

"What woman?" He jerked himself away and fussed with his sweater. She tore his hands loose and took him by the shoulders, her finger nails pinching the flesh.

"Arturo, look at me! You saw him, didn't you?"

"No."

But he smiled; not because he wished to torment her, but because he believed he had succeeded in the lie. Too quickly he smiled. Her mouth closed and her face softened in defeat. She smiled weakly, hating to know yet vaguely pleased that he had tried to shield her from the news.

"I see," she said. "I see."

"You don't see anything, you're talking crazy."

"When did you see him, Arturo?"

"I tell you I didn't."

She straightened herself and drew back her shoulders.

"Go to school, Arturo. I'm all right here. I don't need anybody."

Even so, he remained home, wandering about the house, keeping the stoves fueled, now and then looking into her room, where she lay as always, her glazed eyes studying the ceiling, her beads rattling. She did not urge him to school again, and he felt he was of some use, that she was comforted with his presence. After awhile he pulled a copy of *Horror Crimes* from his hiding place under the floor and sat reading in the kitchen, his feet on a block of wood in the oven.

Always he had wanted his mother to be pretty, to be beautiful. Now it obsessed him, the thought filtering beyond the pages of *Horror Crimes* and shaping itself into the misery of the woman lying on the bed. He put the magazine away and sat biting his lip. Sixteen years ago his mother had been beautiful, for he had seen her picture. Oh that picture! Many times, coming home from school and finding his mother weary and worried and not beautiful, he had gone to the trunk and taken it out—a picture of a large-eyed girl in a wide hat, smiling with so many small teeth, a beauty of a girl standing under the apple tree in Grandma Toscana's backyard. Oh Mamma, to kiss you then! Oh Mamma, why did you change?

Suddenly he wanted to look at that picture again. He hid the pulp and opened the door of the empty room off the kitchen, where his mother's trunk was kept stored. He locked the door from the inside. Huh, and why did he do that ? He unlocked it. The room was like an ice-box. He crossed to the window where the trunk stood. Then he returned and locked the door again. Vaguely he felt he should not be doing this, yet why not : couldn't he even look at a picture of his mother without a sense of evil degrading him ? Well, suppose it wasn't his mother, really : it used to be, so what was the difference ?

Beneath layers of linen and curtains that his mother was saving until 'we get a better house,' beneath ribbons and baby clothes once worn by himself and his brothers, he found the picture. Ah, man ! He held it up and stared at the wonder of that lovely face : here was the mother he had always dreamed about, this girl, no more than twenty, whose eyes he knew resembled his own. Not that weary woman in the other part of the house, she with the thin tortured face, the long bony hands. To have known her then, to have remembered everything from the beginning, to have felt the cradle of that beautiful womb, to have lived remembering from the beginning, and yet he remembered nothing of that time, and always she had been as she was now, weary and with that wistfulness of pain, the great eyes those of someone else, the mouth softer as if from much crying. He traced with his finger the line of her face, kissing it, sighing and murmuring of a past he had never known.

As he put the picture away, his eye fell upon something in one corner of the trunk. It was a tiny jewel box of purple velvet. He had never seen it before. Its presence surprised him, for he had gone through the trunk many times. The little purple box opened when he pressed the spring lock. Inside it, nestling in a silk couch was a black cameo on a gold chain. The dim writing on a card under the silk told him what it was. "For Maria, married one year today. Svevo."

His mind worked fast as he shoved the little box into his pocket and locked the trunk. Rosa, Merry Christmas. A little gift. I bought it, Rosa. I've been saving up for it a long time. For you, Rosa. Merry Christmas.

He was waiting for Rosa next morning at eight o'clock, standing at the water fountain in the hall. It was the last day of classes before Christmas vacation. He knew Rosa always got to school early. Usually he barely made the last bell, running the final two blocks to school. He was sure the nuns who passed regarded him suspiciously, despite their kindly smiles and greetings for a Merry Christmas. In his right coat pocket he felt the snug importance of his gift for Rosa.

By eight-fifteen the kids began to arrive: girls, of course, but no Rosa. He watched the electric clock on the wall. Eight-thirty, and still no Rosa. He frowned with displeasure: a whole half hour spent in school, and for what? For nothing. Sister Celia, her glass eye brighter than the other, swooped downstairs from the convent quarters. Seeing him there on one foot, Arturo who was usually late, she glanced at the watch on her wrist.

"Good heavens! Is my watch stopped?"

She checked with the electric clock on the wall.

"Didn't you go home last night, Arturo?"

"Sure, Sister Celia."

"You mean you deliberately arrived a half hour early this morning?"

"I came to study. Behind in my algebra."

She smiled her doubt. "With Christmas vacation beginning tomorrow?"

"That's right."

But he knew it didn't make sense.

"Merry Christmas, Arturo."

"Ditto, Sister Celia."

Twenty to nine, and no Rosa. Everyone seemed to stare at him, even his brothers, who gaped as though he was in the wrong school, the wrong town.

"Look who's here!"

"Beat it, punk." He bent over to drink some ice water.

At ten of nine she opened the big front door. There she was, red hat, camel's hair coat, zipper overshoes, her face, her whole body lighted up with the cold flame of the winter morning. Nearer and nearer she came, her arms draped lovingly around a great bundle of books. She nodded this way and that to friends, her smile like a melody in that hall: Rosa, president of the Holy Name Girls, everybody's sweetheart coming nearer and nearer in little galoshes that flapped with joy, as though they loved her too.

He tightened the grip around the jewel box. A sudden gusher of blood thundered through his throat. The vivacious sweep of her eyes centered for a fleeting moment upon his tortured ecstatic face, his mouth open, his eyes bulging as he swallowed down his excitement.

He was speechless.

"Rosa . . . I . . . here's . . . ."

Her gaze went past him. The frown became a smile as a classmate rushed up and swept her away. They walked into the cloak room, chattering excitedly. His chest sank. Nuts. He bent over and gulped ice water. Nuts. He spat the water out, hating it, his whole mouth aching. Nuts.

He spent the morning writing notes to Rosa, and tearing them up. Sister Celia had the class read Van Dyke's *The Other Wise Man*. He sat there bored, his mind attuned to the healthier writings found in the pulps.

But when it was Rosa's turn to read he listened as she enunciated with a kind of reverence. Only then did the Van Dyke trash have significance. He knew it was a sin, but he had absolutely no respect for the story of the birth of the Infant Jesus, the flight into Egypt, and the narrative of the child in the manger. But this line of thought was a sin.

During the noon hour, he stalked after her; but she was never alone, always with friends. Once she looked over the shoulders of a girl as a group of them stood in a circle and saw him, as if with a prescience of being followed. He gave up, then, ashamed, and pretended to swagger down the hall. The bell rang and afternoon class began. While Sister Celia talked mysteriously of the Virgin Birth, he wrote more notes to Rosa, tearing them up and writing others. Now he realized he was unequal to the task of presenting the gift to her in person. Someone else would have to do that. The note that satisfied him was:

> *Dear Rosa:*
> *Here is a Merry Xmas*
> *from*
> *Guess Who*

It hurt him when he realized that she would not accept the gift if she recognized the handwriting. With clumsy patience he rewrote it with his left hand, scrawling it in a wild, awkward script. But who would deliver the gift? He studied the faces of classmates around him. None of them, he realized, could possibly keep a secret. He solved the matter by raising two fingers. With the saccharine benevolence of the Christmas season, Sister Celia nodded her permission for him to leave the room. He tiptoed down the side aisle toward the cloak-room.

He recognized Rosa's coat at once, for he was familiar with it, having touched and smelled it on similar occasions. He slipped the note inside the box and dropped the box inside the coat pocket. He embraced the coat, inhaling the fragrance. In the side pocket he found a tiny pair of kid gloves. They were well-worn, the little fingers showing holes.

Aw, jiminy: cute little holes. He kissed them tenderly. Dear little holes in the fingers. Sweet little holes. Don't you cry, cute little holes, you just be brave and keep her fingers warm, her cunning little fingers.

He returned to the classroom, down the side aisle to his seat, his eyes as far away from Rosa as possible, for she must not know, or ever suspect him.

When the dismissal bell rang, he was the first out of the big front doors, running down the street. Tonight he would know if she cared at all, for tonight was the Holy Name Banquet for the Altar Boys. Passing through town, he kept his eyes open for sight of his father, but his watchfulness was unrewarded. He knew he should have remained at school for Altar Boy practice, but that duty had become unbearable with his brother August behind him and the boy across from him, his partner, a miserable fourth grade shrimp.

Reaching home, he was astonished to find a Christmas tree, a small spruce, standing in the corner by the window in the front room. Sipping tea in the kitchen, his mother was apathetic about it.

"I don't know who it was," she said. "A man in a truck."

"What kind of a man, Mamma?"

"A man."

"What kind of a truck?"

"Just a truck."

"What did it say on the truck?"

"I don't know. I didn't pay any attention."

He knew she was lying. He loathed her for this martyr-like acceptance of their plight. She should have thrown the tree back into the man's face. Charity! What did they think his family was—poor? He suspected the Bledsoe family next door: Mrs. Bledsoe, who wouldn't let her Danny and Phillip play with that Bandini boy because he was (1) an Italian, (2) a Catholic, and (3) a bad boy leader of a gang of hoodlums who dumped garbage on her front porch every Hallowe'en. Well, hadn't she sent Danny with a Thanksgiving basket last Thanksgiving, when they didn't need it, and hadn't Bandini ordered Danny to take it back?

"Was it a Salvation Army truck?"

"I don't know.

"Was the man wearing a soldier hat?"

"I don't remember."

"It was the Salvation Army, wasn't it? I bet Mrs. Bledsoe called them up."

"What if it was? Her voice came through her teeth. "I want your father to see that tree. I want him to look at it and see what he's done to us. Even the neighbors know about it. Ah, shame, shame on him."

"To heck with the neighbors."

He walked toward the tree with his fists doubled pugnaciously. "To heck with the neighbors." The tree was about his own height, five feet. He rushed into its prickly fullness and tore at the branches. They had a tender willowy strength, bending and cracking but not breaking. When he had disfigured it to his satisfaction, he threw it into the snow in the front yard. His mother made no protest, staring always into the tea cup, her dark eyes brooding.

"I hope the Bledsoe's see it," he said. "That'll teach them."

"God'll punish him," Maria said. "He will pay for this."

But he was thinking of Rosa, and of what he would wear to the Altar Boy Banquet. He and August and his father always fought about that favorite grey tie, Bandini insisting it was too old for boys, and he and August answering it was too young for a man. Yet somehow it had always remained "Papa's tie," for it had that good father-feeling about it, the front of it showing faint wine-spots and smelling vaguely of Toscanelli cigars. He loved that tie, and he always resented it if he had to wear it immediately after August, for then the mysterious quality of his father was somehow absent from it. He liked his father's handkerchiefs too.

They were so much bigger than his own, and they possessed a softness and a mellowness from being washed and ironed so many times by his mother, and in them he had a vague feeling of his mother and father at the same time. They were unlike the necktie, which was all father, and when he used one of his father's handkerchiefs there came to him dimly a sense of his father and mother together, part of a picture, of a scheme of things.

For a long time he stood before the mirror in his room talking to Rosa, rehearsing his acknowledgment of her thanks. Now he was sure the gift would automatically betray his love. The way he had looked at her that morning, the way he had followed her during the noon hour—she would undoubtedly associate those preliminaries with the jewel. He was glad. He wanted his feelings in the open. He imagined her saying, I knew it was you all the time, Arturo. Standing at the mirror he answered, "Oh well, Rosa, you know how it is, a fellow likes to give his girl a Christmas present."

When his brothers got home at four-thirty he was already dressed. He did not own a complete suit, but Maria always kept his "new" pants and "new" coat neatly pressed. They did not match, but they came pretty close to it, the pants of blue serge and the coat an oxford grey.

The change into his "new" clothes transformed him into a picture of frustration and misery as he sat in the rocking chair, his hands folded in his lap. The only thing he ever did when he got into his "new" clothes, and he always did it badly, was simply to sit and wait out the period to the bitter end. Now he had four hours to wait before the banquet began, but there was some consolation in the fact that tonight, at least, he would not eat eggs.

When August and Federico let loose a barrage of questions about the broken Christmas tree in the front yard, his "new" clothes seemed tighter than ever. The night was going to be warm and clear, so he pulled on one sweater over his grey coat instead of two and left, glad to be away from the gloom of home.

Walking down the street in that shadow-world of black and white he felt the serenity of impending victory: the smile of Rosa tonight, his gift around her neck as she waited on the Altar Boys in the auditorium, her smiles for him and for him alone.

Ah, what a night!

He talked to himself as he walked, breathing the thin mountain air, reeling in the glory of his possessions, Rosa my girl, Rosa for me and for nobody else. Only one thing disturbed him, and that vaguely: he was hungry, but the emptiness in his stomach was dissipated by the overflow of his joy. These Altar Boy Banquets, and he had attended seven of them in his life, were supreme achievements in food. He could see it all before him, huge plates of fried chicken and turkey, hot buns, sweet potatoes, cranberry sauce, and all the chocolate ice cream he could eat, and beyond it all, Rosa with a cameo around her neck, his gift, smiling as he gorged himself, serving him with bright black eyes and teeth so white they were good enough to eat.

What a night! He bent down and snatched at the white snow, letting it melt in his mouth, the cold liquid trickling down his throat. He did this many times, sucking the sweet snow and enjoying the cold effect in his throat.

The intestinal reaction to the cold liquid on his empty stomach was a faint purring somewhere in the middle of him and rising toward the cardiac area. He was crossing the trestle bridge, in the very middle of it, when everything before his eyes melted suddenly into blackness. His feet lost all sensory response. His breath came in frantic jerks. He found himself flat on his back. He had fallen over limply. Deep within his chest his heart hammered for movement. He clutched it with both hands, terror gripping him. He was dying: oh God, he was going to die! The very bridge seemed to shake with the violence of his heart beat.

But five, ten, twenty seconds later he was still alive. The terror of that moment still burned in his heart. What had happened? Why had he fallen? He got up and hurried across the trestle bridge, shivering in fear. What had he done? It was his heart, he knew his heart had stopped beating and started again—but why?

Mea culpa, mea culpa, mea maxima culpa! The mysterious universe loomed around him, and he was alone on the railroad tracks, hurrying to the street where men and women walked, where it was not so lonely, and as he ran it came to him like piercing daggers that this was God's warning, this was His way of letting him know that God knew his crime: he, the thief, filcher of his mother's cameo, sinner against the decalogue. Thief, thief, outcast of God, hell's child with a black mark across the book of his soul.

It might happen again. Now, five minutes from now. Ten minutes. Hail Mary full of grace I'm sorry. He no longer ran but walked now, briskly, almost running dreading over-excitation of his heart. Goodbye to Rosa and thoughts of love, goodbye and goodbye, and hello to sorrow and remorse.

Ah, the cleverness of God! Ah, how good the Lord was to him, giving him another chance, warning him yet not killing him.

Look! See how I walk. I breathe. I am alive. I am walking to God. My soul is black. God will clean my soul. He is good to me. My feet touch the ground, one two, one two. I'll call Father Andrew. I'll tell him everything.

He rang the bell on the Confessional wall. Five minutes later Father Andrew appeared through the side door of the church. The tall, semi-bald priest raised his eyebrows in surprise to find but one soul in that Christmas decorated church—and that soul a boy, his eyes tightly closed, his jaws gritted, his lips moving in prayer. The priest smiled, removed the tooth-pick from his mouth, genuflected, and walked toward the Confessional. Arturo opened his eyes and saw him advancing like a thing of beautiful black, and there was comfort in his presence, and warmth in his black cassock.

"What now, Arturo?" he said in a whisper that was pleasant. He laid his hand on Arturo's shoulder. It was like the touch of God. His agony broke beneath it. The vagueness of nascent peace stirred within depths, ten million miles within him.

"I gotta' go to confession, Father."

"Sure, Arturo."

Father Andrew adjusted his sash and entered the Confessional door. He followed, kneeling in the penitent's booth, the wooden screen separating him from the priest. After the prescribed ritual, he said: "Yesterday, Father Andrew, I was going through my mother's trunk, and I found a cameo with a gold chain, and I swiped it, Father. I put it in my pocket, and it didn't belong to me, it belonged to my mother, my father gave it to her, and it musta' been worth a lot of money, but I swiped it anyhow, and today I gave it to a girl in our school. I gave stolen property for a Christmas present."

"You say it was valuable?" the priest asked.

"It looked it," he answered.

"How valuable, Arturo ?"

"It looked plenty valuable, Father. I'm awfully sorry, Father. I'll never steal again as long as I live."

"Tell you what, Arturo," the priest said. I'll give you absolution if you'll promise to go to your mother and tell her you stole the cameo. Tell her just as you've told me. If she prizes it, and wants it back, you've got to promise me you'll get it from the girl, and return it to your mother. Now if you can't do that, you've got to promise me you'll buy your mother another one. Isn't that fair, Arturo ? I think God'll agree that you're getting a square deal."

"I'll get it back. I'll try."

He bowed his head while the priest mumbled the Latin of absolution. That was all. Easy as pie. He left the Confessional and knelt in the church, his hands pressed over his heart. It thumped serenely. He was saved. It was a swell world after all. For a long time he knelt, reveling in the sweetness of escape. They were pals, he and God, and God was a good sport. But he took no chances. For two hours, until the clock struck eight, he prayed every prayer he knew. Everything was coming out fine. The priest's advice was a cinch. Tonight after the banquet he would tell his mother the truth—that he had stolen her cameo and given it to Rosa. She would protest at first. But not for long. He knew his mother, and how to get things out of her.

He crossed the schoolyard and climbed the stairs to the auditorium. In the hall the first person he saw was Rosa. She walked directly to him.

"I want to talk to you," she said.

"Sure, Rosa."

He followed her downstairs, fearful that something awful was about to happen. At the bottom of the stairs she waited for him to open the door, her jaw set, her camel's hair coat wrapped tightly around her.

"I'm sure hungry," he said.

"Are you?" Her voice was cold, supercilious.

They stood on the stairs outside the door, at the edge of the concrete platform. She held out her hand.

"Here," she said. "I don't want this."

It was the cameo.

"I can't accept stolen property," she said. "My mother says you probably stole this."

"I didn't!" he lied. "I did not!"

"Take it," she said. "I don't want it."

He put it in his pocket. Without a word she turned to enter the building.

"But Rosa!"

At the door she turned around and smiled sweetly.

"You shouldn't steal, Arturo."

"I *didn't* steal!" He sprang at her, dragged her out of the doorway and pushed her. She backed to the edge of the platform and toppled into the snow, after swaying and waving her arms in a futile effort to get her balance. As she landed her mouth opened wide and let out a scream.

"I'm *not* a thief," he said looking down at her.

He jumped from the platform to the sidewalk and hurried away as fast as he could. At the corner he looked at the cameo for a moment, and then tossed it with all his might over the roof of the two-story house bordering the street. Then he walked on again. To hell with the Altar Boy Banquet. He wasn't hungry anyway.

7.

CHRISTMAS EVE. SVEVO BANDINI WAS COMING home, new shoes on his feet, defiance in his jaw, guilt in his heart. Fine shoes, Bandini; where'd you get them? None of your business. He had money in his pocket. His fist squeezed it. Where'd you get that money, Bandini? Playing poker. I've been playing it for ten days.

Indeed!

But that was his story, and if his wife didn't believe, what of it? His black shoes smashed the snow, the sharp new heels chopping it.

They were expecting him: somehow they knew he would arrive. The very house had a feeling for it. Things were in order. Maria by the window spoke her rosary very fast, as though there was so little time: a few more prayers before he arrived.

Merry Christmas. The boys had opened their gifts. They

each had one gift. Pajamas from Grandma Toscana. They sat around in their pajamas—waiting. For what? The suspense was good: something was going to happen. Pajamas of blue and green. They had put them on because there was nothing else to do. But something was going to happen. In the silence of waiting it was wonderful to think that Papa was coming home, and not speak of it.

Federico had to spoil it.

"I bet Papa's coming home tonight."

A break in the spell. It was a private thought belonging to each. Silence. Federico regretted his words and fell to wondering why they had not answered.

A footstep on the porch. All the men and women on earth could have mounted that step, yet none would have made a sound like that. They looked at Maria. She held her breath, hurrying through one more prayer. The door opened and he came inside. He closed the door carefully, as though his whole life had been spent in the exact science of closing doors.

"Hello."

He was no boy caught stealing marbles, nor a dog punished for tearing up a shoe. This was Svevo Bandini, a full-grown man with a wife and three sons.

"Where's Mamma?" he said, looking right at her, like a drunken man who wanted to prove he could ask a serious question. Over in the corner he saw her, exactly where he knew she was, for he had been frightened by her silhouette from the street.

"Ah, there she is."

I hate you, she thought. With my fingers I want to tear out your eyes and blind you. You are a beast, you have hurt me and I shall not rest until I have hurt you.

Papa with new shoes. They squeaked with his step as though tiny mice ran around in them. He crossed the room to the bathroom. Strange sound—old Papa home again.

I hope you die. You will never touch me again. I hate you, God what have you done to me, my husband, I hate you so.

He came back and stood in the middle of the room, his back to his wife. From his pocket he extracted the money. And to his sons he said, "Suppose we all go downtown before the stores close, you and me and Mamma, all of us, and go down and buy some Christmas presents for everybody."

"I want a bicycle!" from Federico.

"Sure. You get a bicycle!"

Arturo didn't know what he wanted, nor did August. The evil he had done twisted inside Bandini, but he smiled and said they would find something for all. A big Christmas. The biggest of all.

I can see that other woman in his arms, I can smell her in his clothes, her lips have roamed his face, her hands have explored his chest. He disgusts me, and I want him hurt to death.

"And what'll we get Mamma?"

He turned around and faced her, his eyes on the money as he unrolled the bills.

"Look at all the money! Better give it all to Mamma, huh? All the money Papa won playing cards. Pretty good card-player, Papa."

He raised his eyes and looked at her, she with her hands gripped in the sides of the chair, as though ready to spring at him, and he realized he was afraid of her, and he smiled not in amusement but fear, the evil he had done weakening his courage. Fan-wise he held the money out: there were fives and tens, a hundred even, and like a condemned man going to his punishment he kept the silly smile on his lips as he bent over and made to hand her the bills, trying to think of the old words, their words, his and hers, their language. She clung to the chair in horror forcing herself not to shrink back from the serpent of guilt that wound itself into the ghastly figure of his face. Closer than ever he bent, only inches from her hair, utterly ridiculous in his ameliorations, until she could not bear it, could not refrain from it, and with a suddenness that surprised her too, her ten long fingers were at his eyes, tearing down, a singing strength in her ten long fingers that laid streaks of blood down his face as he screamed and backed away, the front of his shirt, his neck and collar gathering the fast-falling red drops. But it was his eyes, my God my eyes, my eyes!

And he backed away and covered them with his cupped hands, standing against the wall, his face reeking with pain, afraid to lift his hands, afraid that he was blind.

"Maria," he sobbed. "Oh God, what have you done to me?"

He could see; dimly through a curtain of red he could see, and he staggered around.

"Ah Maria, what have you done? What have you done?"

Around the room he staggered. He heard the weeping of his children, the words of Arturo: "Oh God." Around and round he staggered, blood and tears in his eyes.

"*Jesu Christi*, what has happened to me?"

At his feet lay the green bills and he staggered through them and upon them in his new shoes, little red drops splattered over the shining black toes, round and round, moaning and groping his way to the door and outside into the cold night, into the snow, deep into the drift in the yard moaning all the time, his big hands scooping snow like water and pressing it to his burning face. Again and again the white snow from his hands fell back to the earth, red and sodden. In the house his sons stood petrified, in their new pajamas, the front door open, the light in the middle of the room blinding their view of Svevo Bandini as he blotted his face with the linen of the sky. In the chair sat Maria. She did not move as she stared at the blood and the money strewn about the room.

Damn her, Auturo thought. Damn her to hell.

He was crying, hurt by the humiliation of his father; his father, that man, always so solid and powerful, and he had seen him floundering and hurt and crying, his father who never cried and never floundered. He wanted to be with his father, and he put on his shoes and hurried outside, where Bandini was bent over, choked and quivering. But it was good to hear something over and above the choking—to hear his anger, his curses. It thrilled him when he heard his father vowing vengeance. I'll kill her, by God, I'll kill her. He was gaining control of himself now. The snow had checked the flow of blood. He stood panting, examining his bloody clothes, his hands spattered crimson.

"Somebody's got to pay for this," he said. *"Sangue de la Madonna!* It shall not be forgotten."

"Papa—"

"What do you want?"

"Nothing."

"Then get in the house. Get in there with that crazy mother of yours."

That was all. He broke his way through the snow to the sidewalk and strode down the street. The boy watched him go, his face high to the night. It was the way he walked, stumbling despite his determination. But no—after a few feet he turned, "You kids have a happy Christmas. Take that money and go down and buy what you want."

He went on again, his chin out, coasting into the cold air, bearing up under a deep wound that was not bleeding.

The boy went back to the house. The money was not on the floor. One look at Federico, who choked bitterly as he held out a torn section of a five dollar bill told him what had happened. He opened the stove. The black embers of burnt paper smoked faintly. He closed the stove and examined the floor, bare except for drying blood spots. In hatred he glared at his mother. She did not move or even heed with her eyes, but her lips opened and shut, for she had resumed her rosary.

"Merry Christmas!" he sneered.

Federico wailed. August was too shocked to speak.

Yea: a Merry Chistmas. Ah, give it to her Papa! Me and you, Papa, because I know how you feel, because it happened to me too, but you should have done what I did Papa, knocked her down like I did, and you'd feel better. Because you're killing me, Papa, you with your bloody face walking around all by yourself, you're killing me.

He went out on the porch and sat down. The night was full of his father. He saw the red spots in the snow where Bandini had floundered and bent to lift it to his face. Papa's blood, my blood. He stepped off the porch and kicked clean snow over the place until it disappeared. Nobody should see this: nobody. Then he returned to the house.

His mother had not moved. How he hated her! With one

grasp he tore the rosary out of her hands and pulled it to pieces. She watched him, martyrlike. She got up and followed him outside, the broken rosary in his fist. He threw it far out into the snow, scattering it like seeds. She walked past him into the snow.

In astonishment he watched her wade knee-deep into the whiteness, gazing around like one dazed. Here and there she found a bead, her hand cupping fistfuls of snow. It disgusted him. She was pawing the very spot where his father's blood had colored the snow.

Hell with her. He was leaving. He wanted his father. He dressed and walked down the street. Merry Christmas. The town was painted green and white with it. A hundred dollars in the stove—but what about him, his brothers? You could be holy and firm, but why must they all suffer? His mother had too much God in her.

Where now? He didn't know, but not at home with her. He could understand his father. A man had to do something: never having anything was too monotonous. He had to admit it: if *he* could choose between Maria and Effie Hildegarde, it would be Effie every time. When Italian women got to a certain age their legs thinned and their bellies widened, their breasts fell and they lost sparkle. He tried to imagine Rosa Pinelli at forty. Her legs would thin like his mother's; she would be fat in the stomach. But he could not imagine it. That Rosa, so lovely! He wished instead that she would die. He pictured disease wasting her away until there had to be a funeral. It would make him happy. He would go to her death-bed and stand over it. She would weakly take his hand in her hot fingers and tell him she was going to die, and he would answer, too bad Rosa; you had your chance, but I'll always remember you Rosa. Then the funeral, the weeping, and Rosa lowered into the earth. But he would be cold to it all, stand there and smile a little with his great dreams. Years later in the Yankee stadium, over the yells of the crowd he'd remember a dying girl who held his hand and begged forgiveness; only for a few seconds would he linger with that memory, and then he would turn to the women in the crowd and nod, his women, not an Italian among them; blondes they'd be, tall and smiling, dozens of them, like Effie Hildegarde, and not an Italian in the lot.

So give it to her Papa! I'm for you, old boy. Some day I'll be doing it too, I'll be right in there some day with a honey like her, and she won't be the kind that scratches my face, and she won't be the kind that calls me a little thief.

And yet, how did he know that Rosa *wasn't* dying? Of course she was, just as all people moved minute by minute nearer the grave. But just suppose, just for the heck of it, that Rosa really was dying! What about his friend Joe Tanner last year? Killed riding a bicycle; one day he was alive, the next he wasn't. And what about Nellie Frazier?

A little stone in her shoe; she didn't take it out; blood-poison, and all at once she was dead and they had a funeral.

How did he know that Rosa hadn't been run over by an automobile since he saw her that last awful time? There was a chance. How did he know she wasn't dead by electrocution? That happened a lot. Why couldn't it happen to her? Of course he really didn't want her to die, not really and truly cross my heart and hope to die, but still and all there was a chance. Poor Rosa, so young and pretty—and dead.

He was downtown, walking around, nothing there, only people hurrying with packages. He was in front of Wilkes Hardware Company, staring at the sports display. It began to snow. He looked to the mountains. They were blotted by black clouds. An odd premonition took hold of him: Rosa Pinelli was dead. He was positive she was dead. All he had to do was walk three blocks down Pearl Street and two blocks east on Twelfth Street and it would be proven. He could walk there and on the front door of the Pinelli house there would be a funeral wreath. He was so sure of it that he walked in that direction at once. Rosa was dead. He was a prophet, given to understanding weird things. And so it had finally happened: what he wished had come true, and she was gone.

Well, well, funny world. He lifted his eyes to the sky, to the millions of snowflakes floating earthward. The end of

Rosa Pinelli. He spoke aloud, addressing imagined listeners. I was standing in front of Wilkes Hardware, and all of a sudden I had that hunch. Then I walked up to her house, and sure enough, there was a wreath on the door. A swell kid, Rosa. Sure hate to see her die. He hurried now, the premonition weakening, and he walked faster, speeding to outlast it. He was crying: Oh Rosa, please don't die, Rosa. Be alive when I get there! Here I come Rosa, my love. All the way from the Yankee stadium in a chartered airplane. I made a landing right on the court house lawn—nearly killed three hundred people out there watching me. But I made it, Rosa. I got here all right, and here I am at your bedside, just in time, and the doctor says you'll live now, and so I must go away, never to return. Back to the Yanks, Rosa. To Florida, Rosa. Spring training. The Yanks need me too; but you'll know where I am, Rosa, just read the papers and you'll know.

There was no funeral wreath on the Pinelli door. What he saw there, and he gasped in horror until his vision cleared through the blinding snow, was a Christmas wreath instead. He was glad, hurrying away in the storm. Sure I'm glad! Who wants to see anybody die? But he wasn't glad, he wasn't glad at all. He wasn't a star for the Yankees. He hadn't come by chartered plane. He wasn't going to Florida. This was Christmas Eve in Rocklin, Colorado. It was snowing like the devil, and his father was living with a woman named Effie Hildegarde. His father's face was torn open by his mother's fingers and at that moment he knew his mother was praying, his brothers were crying, and the embers in the front room stove had once been a hundred dollars.

Merry Christmas, Arturo!

8

A LONELY ROAD AT THE WEST END OF ROCK-
lin, thin and dwindling, the falling snow strangling it. Now
the snow falls heavily. The road creeps westward and upward, a steep road. Beyond are the mountains. The snow!
It chokes the world, and there is a pale void ahead, only the
thin road dwindling fast. A tricky road, full of surprising
twists and dips as it eludes the dwarfed pines standing with
hungry white arms to capture it.

Maria, what have you done to Svevo Bandini? What have
you done to my face?

A square-built man stumbling along, his shoulders and
arms covered by the snow. In this place the road is steep;
he breasts his way, the deep snow pulling at his legs, a man
wading through water that has not melted.

Where now, Bandini?

A little while ago, not more than forty-five minutes, he

had come rushing down this road, convinced that, as God was his judge, he would never return again. Forty-five minutes—not even an hour, and much had happened, and he was returning along a road that he had hoped might be forgotten.

Maria, what have you done?

Svevo Bandini, a blood-tinted handkerchief concealing his face, and the wrath of Winter concealing Svevo Bandini as he climbed the road back to the Widow Hildegarde's, talking to the snow-flakes as he climbed. So tell the snow-flakes, Bandini; tell them as you wave your cold hands. Bandini sobbed—a grown man, forty-two years old, weeping because it was Christmas Eve and he was returning to his sin, because he would rather be with his children.

Maria, what have you done?

It was like this, Maria: ten days ago your mother wrote that letter, and I got mad and left the house, because I can't stand the woman. I must go away when she comes. And so I went away. I got lots of troubles, Maria. The kids. The house. The snow: look at the snow tonight, Maria. Can I set a brick down in it? And I'm worried, and your mother is coming, and I say to myself, I say, I think I'll go downtown and have a few drinks. Because I got troubles. Because I got kids.

Ah, Maria.

He had gone downtown to the Imperial Poolhall, and

there he had met his friend Rocco Saccone, and Rocco had said they should go to his room and have a drink, smoke a cigar, talk. Old friends, he and Rocco: two men in a room filled with cigar smoke drinking whiskey on a cold day, talking. Christmas Time: a few drinks. Happy Christmas, Svevo. Gratia, Rocco. A happy Christmas.

Rocco had looked at the face of his friend and asked what troubled him, and Bandini had told him: no money, Rocco, the kids and Christmas time. And the mother-in-law—damn her. Rocco was a poor man too, not so poor as Bandini, though, and he offered ten dollars. How could Bandini accept it? Already he had borrowed so much from his friend, and now this. No thanks, Rocco. I drink your liquor, that's enough. And so, *a la salute!* for old times sake . . .

One drink and then another, two men in a room with their feet on the steaming radiator. Then the buzzer above Rocco's hotel room door sounded. Once, and then once more: the telephone. Rocco jumped up and hurried down the hall to the phone. After awhile he returned, his face soft and pleasant. Rocco got many phone calls in the hotel, for he ran an advertisement in the *Rocklin Herald*:

> Rocco Saccone, bricklayer and
> stonemason. All kinds of re-
> pair work. Concrete work a
> specialty. Call R.M. Hotel.

That was it, Maria. A woman named Hildegarde had

called Rocco and told him that her fireplace was out of order. Would Rocco come and fix it right away?

Rocco, his friend.

"You go, Svevo," he said. "Maybe you can make a few dollars before Xmas."

That was how it started. With Rocco's tool sack on his back, he left the hotel, crossed the town to the West end, took this very road on a late afternoon ten days ago. Up this very road, and he remembered a chipmunk standing under that very tree over there, watching him as he passed. A few dollars to fix a fireplace; maybe three hours' work, maybe more—a few dollars.

The Widow Hildegarde? Of course he knew who she was, but who in Rocklin did not? A town of ten thousand people, and one woman owning most of the land—who among those ten thousand could avoid knowing her? But who had never known her well enough to say hello, and that was the truth.

This very road, ten days ago, with a bit of cement and seventy pounds of mason's tools on his back. That was the first time he saw the Hildegarde cottage, a famous place around Rocklin because the stone work was so fine. Coming upon it in the late afternoon, that low house built of white flagstone and set among tall pine trees seemed a place out of his dreams: an irresistible place, the kind he would some day have, if he could afford it. For a long time he stood gazing and gazing upon it, wishing he might have had some hand in its construction, the delight of masonry, of handling those long white stones, so soft beneath a mason's hands, yet strong enough to outlast a civilization.

What does a man think about when he approaches the white door to such a house and reaches for the polished foxhead brass knocker?

Wrong, Maria.

He had never talked to the woman until that moment she opened the door. A woman taller than himself, round and large. Aye: fine-looking woman. Not like Maria, but still a fine-looking woman. Dark hair, blue eyes, a woman who looked as though she had money.

His sack of tools gave him away.

So he was Rocco Saccone, the mason. How do you do?

No, but he was Rocco's friend. Rocco was ill.

It didn't matter who he was, so long as he could fix a fireplace. Come in Mr. Bandini, the fireplace is over there. And so he entered, his hat in one hand, the sack of tools in the other. A beautiful house, Indian rugs over the floor, large beams across the ceiling, the woodwork done in bright yellow lacquer. It might have cost twenty—even thirty thousand dollars.

There are things a man cannot tell his wife. Would Maria understand that surge of humility as he crossed the handsome room, the embarrassment as he staggered when his worn shoes, wet with snow, failed to grip the shining yellow floor ? Could he tell Maria that the attractive woman felt a sudden pity for him ? It was true : even though his back was turned, he felt the Widow's quick embarrassment for him, for his awkward strangeness.

"Pretty slippery, ain't it ?"

The Widow laughed. "I'm always falling."

But that was to help him cover his embarrassment. A little thing, a courtesy to make him feel at home.

Nothing seriously wrong with the fireplace, a few loose brick in the flue-lining, a matter of an hour's work. But there are tricks to the trade, and the Widow was wealthy. Drawing himself up after the inspection, he told her the work would amount to fifteen dollars, including the price of materials. She did not object. Then it came to him as a sickening afterthought that the reason for her liberality was the condition of his shoes: she had seen the worn soles as he knelt to examine the fireplace. Her way of looking at him, up and down, that pitying smile, possessed an understanding that had sent the Winter through his flesh. He could not tell Maria that.

Sit down, Mr. Bandini.

He found the deep reading chair voluptuously comfortable, a chair from the Widow's world, and he stretched out in it and surveyed the bright room cluttered neatly with books and bric-a-brac. An educated woman ensconced in the luxury of her education. She was seated on the divan, her plump legs in their sheer silk cases, rich legs that swished of silk when she crossed them before his wondering eyes. She asked him to sit and talk with her. He was so grateful that he could not speak, could only utter happy grunts at whatever she said, her rich precise words flowing from her deep luxurious throat. He fell to wondering about her, his eyes bulging with curiosity for her protected world, so sleek and bright, like the rich silk that defined the round luxury of her handsome legs.

Maria would scoff if she knew what the Widow talked about, for he found his throat too tight, too choked with the strangeness of the scene: she, over there, the wealthy Mrs. Hildegarde, worth a hundred, maybe two hundred thousand dollars, and not more than four feet away—so close that he might have leaned over and touched her.

So he was an Italian? Splendid. Only last year she had traveled in Italy. Beautiful. He must be so proud of his heritage. Did he know that the cradle of western civilization was Italy? Had he ever seen the Campo Santo, the Cathedral of St. Peter's, the paintings of Michelangelo, the blue Mediterranean? The Italian Riviera?

No, he had seen none of these. In simple words he told her that he was from Abruzzi, that he had never been that far North, never to Rome. He had worked hard as a boy. There had been no time for anything else.

Abruzzi! The Widow knew everything. Then surely he had read the works of D'Annunzio—he, too, was an Abruzzian.

No, he had not read D'Annunzio. He had heard of him, but he had never read him. Yes, he knew the great man was from his own province. It pleased him. It made him grateful to D'Annunzio. Now they had something in common, but to his dismay he found himself unable to say more on the subject. For a full minute the Widow watched him, her blue eyes expressionless as they centered on his lips. He turned his head in confusion, his gaze following the heavy beams across the room, the frilled curtains, the nicknacks spread in careful profusion everywhere.

A kind woman, Maria: a good woman who came to his rescue and made conversation easy. Did he like to lay brick? Did he have a family? Three children? Wonderful. She, too, had wanted children. Was his wife an Italian, too? Had he lived in Rocklin long?

The weather. She spoke of the weather. Ah. He spoke then tumbling out his torment at the weather. Almost whining he lamented his stagnation, his fierce hatred of cold sunless days. Until, frightened by his bitter torrent, she glanced at her watch and told him to come back to-morrow morning to begin work on the fireplace. At the door, hat in hand, he stood waiting for her parting words.

"Put on your hat, Mr. Bandini," she smiled. "You'll catch

cold." Grinning, his armpits and neck flooded with nervous sweat, he pulled his hat down, confused and at a loss for words.

He stayed with Rocco that night. With Rocco, Maria, not with the Widow. The next day, after ordering firebrick at the lumber yard, he went back to the Widow's cottage to repair the fireplace. Spreading a canvas over the carpet, he mixed his mortar in a bucket, tore out the loose brick in the flue-lining, and laid new brick in their place. Determined that the job should last a full day, he pulled out all the firebrick. He might have finished in an hour, might have pulled out only two or three, but at noon he was only half through. Then the Widow appeared, coming quietly from one of the sweet-scented rooms. Again the flutter in his throat. Again he could do no more than smile. How was he getting along with the work? He had done a careful job: not a speck of mortar smeared the faces of the brick he had laid. Even the canvas was clean, the old brick piled neatly at the side. She noticed this, and it pleased him. No passion lured him as she stooped to examine the new brick inside the fireplace, her sleek girdled bottom so rounded as she sank to her haunches. No Maria, not even her high heels, her thin blouse, the fragrance of the perfume in her dark hair, moved him to a stray thought of infidelity. As before he watched her in wonder and curiosity: this woman with a hundred, maybe two hundred thousand in the bank.

His plan to go downtown for lunch was unthinkable. As soon as she heard it she insisted that he remain as her guest. His eyes could not meet the cold blue of hers. He bowed his head, pawed the canvas with one toe, and begged to be excused. Eat lunch with the Widow Hildegarde? Sit across the table from her and put food in his mouth while this woman sat opposite him? He could scarcely breathe his refusal.

"No, no. Please, Mrs. Hildegarde, thank you. Thank you so much. Please, no. Thank you."

But he stayed, not daring to offend her. Smiling as he held out his mortar-caked hands, he asked her if he might wash them, and she led him through the white, spotless hall to the bathroom. The room was like a jewel-box: shining yellow tile, the yellow washbowl, lavender organdie curtains over the tall window, a bowl of purple flowers on the mirrored dressing table, yellow-handled perfume bottles, yellow comb-and-brush set. He turned quickly and all but bolted away. He could not have been more shocked had she stood naked before him. Those grimy hands of his were unworthy of this. He preferred the kitchen sink, just as he did at home. But her ease reassured him, and he entered fearfully, on the balls of his feet, and stood before the washbowl with tortured indecision. With his elbow he turned the water spout, afraid to mark it with his fingers. The scented green soap was out of the question: he did the best he could with water alone. When he finished, he dried his hands on the tail of his shirt, ignoring the soft green towels that hung from the wall. The experience left him fearful of what might take place at lunch. Before leaving the bathroom, he got down on his knees and blotted up a spot or two of splashed water with his shirt sleeve. . . .

A lunch of lettuce leaves, pineapple and cottage cheese. Seated in the breakfast nook, a pink napkin across his knees, he ate with a suspicion that it was a joke, that the Widow was making fun of him. But she ate it too, and with such gusto that it might have been palatable. If Maria had served him such food, he would have thrown it out the window. Then the Widow brought tea in a thin China cup. There were two white cookies in the saucer, no larger than the end of his thumb. Tea and cookies. *Diavolo!* He had always identified tea with effeminacy and weakness, and he had no liking for sweets. But the Widow, munching a cookie between two fingers, smiled graciously as he tossed the cakes in his mouth like one putting away unpleasant pills.

Long before she finished her second cookie he was done, had drained the teacup, and leaned back on the two rear legs of his chair, his stomach mewing and crowing its protest at such strange visitors. They had not spoken throughout the lunch, not a word. It made him conscious that there was nothing to say between them. Now and then she smiled, once over the rim of her teacup. It left him embarrassed and sad: the life of the rich, he concluded, was not for him. At home he would have eaten fried eggs, a chunk of bread, and washed it down with a glass of wine.

When she finished, touching the corners of her carmine lips with the tip of her napkin, she asked if there was anything else he would like. His impulse was to answer, "What else you got?" but he patted his stomach instead, puffing it out and caressing it.

"No, thank you, Mrs. Hildegarde. I'm full—full clean up to the ears."

It made her smile. With red knotted fists at his belt, he remained leaning backward in his chair, sucking his teeth and craving a cigar.

A fine woman, Maria. One who sensed his every desire.

"Do you smoke?" she asked, producing a pack of cigarettes from the table drawer. From his shirt pocket he pulled the butt of a twisted Toscanelli cigar, bit off the end and spat it across the floor, lighted a match and puffed away. She insisted that he remain where he was, comfortable and at ease, while she gathered the dishes, the cigarette dangling from the corner of her mouth. The cigar eased his tension. Crossing his arms, he watched her more frankly, studying the sleek hips, the soft white arms. Even then his thought was clean, no vagabond sensuality clouding his mind. She was a rich woman and he was near her, seated in her kitchen; he was grateful for the proximity:

· 181 ·

for that and for nothing more, as God was his judge.

Finishing his cigar, he went back to his work. By four-thirty he was finished. Gathering his tools, he waited for her to come into the room again. All afternoon he had heard her in another part of the house. For some time he waited, clearing his throat loudly, dropping his trowel, singing a tune with the words, "It's finished, oh it's all done, all finished, all finished." The commotion at last brought her to the room. She came with a book in her hand, wearing reading glasses. He expected to be paid immediately. Instead he was surprised when she asked him to sit down for a moment. She did not even glance at the work he had done.

"You're a splendid worker, Mr. Bandini. Splendid. I'm very pleased."

Maria might sneer, but those words almost pinched a tear from his eyes. "I do, my best, Mrs. Hildegarde. I do the best I can."

But she showed no desire to pay him. Once more the whitish-blue eyes. Their clear appraisal caused him to shift his glance to the fireplace. The eyes remained upon him, studying him vaguely, trance-like, as if she had lapsed into a reverie of other things. He walked to the fireplace and put his eye along the mantel-piece, as if to gauge its angle, pursing his lips with that look of mathematical computation. When he had done this until it could no longer seem sensible, he returned to the deep chair and seated himself once more. The Widow's gaze followed him mechanically. He wanted to speak, but what was there to say?

At last she broke the silence: she had other work for him. There was a house of hers in town, on Windsor Street. There, too, the fireplace was not functioning. Would he go there tomorrow and examine it? She arose, crossed the room to the writing desk by the window, and wrote down the address. Her back was to him, her body bent at the waist, her round hips blooming sensuously, and though Maria might tear out his very eyes and spit into their empty sockets, he could swear that no evil had darkened his glance, no lust had lurked in his heart.

That night, lying in the darkness beside Rocco Saccone, the wailing snores of his friend keeping him awake, there was yet another reason why Svevo Bandini did not sleep, and that was the promise of tomorrow. He lay grunting contentedly in the darkness. *Mannaggia,* he was no fool; he was wise enough to realize he had made his mark with the Widow Hildegarde. She might pity him, she might have given him this new job only because she felt that he needed it, but whatever it was, there was no question of his ability; she had called him a splendid worker, and rewarded him with more work.

Let the Winter blow! Let the temperature drop to freezing. Let the snow pile up and bury the town! He didn't care: tomorrow there was work. And after that, there would always be work. The Widow Hildegarde liked him; she respected his ability. With her money and his ability there would always be work enough to laugh at the Winter.

At seven the next morning he entered the house on Windsor Street. No one lived in the house; the front door was open when he tried it. No furniture: only bare rooms. Nor could he find anything wrong with the fireplace. It was not so elaborate as the one at the Widow's but it was well-made. The mortar had not cracked, and the brick responded solidly to the tapping of his hammer. Then what was it? He found wood in the shed in the rear and built a fire. The flue sucked the flame voraciously. Heat filled the room. Nothing wrong.

Eight o'clock, and he was at the Widow's again. In a blue dressing gown he found her, fresh and smiling her good morning. Mr. Bandini! But you mustn't stand out there in the cold. Come inside and have a cup of coffee! The protests died on his lips. He kicked the snow from his wet shoes and followed the flowing blue gown to the kitchen. Standing against the sink, he drank the coffee, pouring it into a saucer and then blowing on it to cool it. He did not look at her below the shoulders. He dared not. Maria would never believe that. Nervous and without speech, he behaved like a man.

He told her that he could find no trouble with the Windsor

Street fireplace. His honesty pleased him, coming as it did after the exaggerated work of the day before. The Widow seemed surprised. She was certain there was something wrong with the Windsor Street fireplace. She asked him to wait while she dressed. She would drive him back to Windsor Street and show him the trouble. Now she was staring at his wet feet.

"Mr. Bandini, don't you wear a size nine shoe?"

The blood rose to his face, and he sputtered in his coffee. Quickly she apologized. It was the outstanding bad habit of her life—this obsession she had of asking people what size shoe they wore. It was a sort of guessing game she played with herself. Would he forgive her?

The episode shook him deeply. To hide his shame he quickly seated himself at the table, his wet shoes beneath it, out of view. But the Widow smiled and persisted. Had she guessed right? Was size nine correct?

"Sure is, Mrs. Hildegarde."

Waiting for her to dress, Svevo Bandini felt that he was getting somewhere in the world. From now on Helmer the banker and all his creditors had better be careful. Bandini had powerful friends too.

But what had he to hide of that day? No—he was proud of that day. Beside the Widow, in her car, he rode through the middle of town, down Pearl Street, the Widow at the wheel in a seal skin coat. Had Maria and his children seen him chatting easily with her, they would have been proud of him. They might have proudly raised their chins and said, there goes our Papa! But Maria had torn the flesh from his face.

What happened in the vacant house on Windsor Street? Did he lead the Widow to a vacant room and violate her? Did he kiss her? Then go to that house, Maria. Speak to the cold rooms. Scoop the cobwebs from the corners and ask them questions; ask the naked floors, ask the frosted window panes; ask them if Svevo Bandini had done wrong.

The Widow stood before the fireplace.

"You see," he said. "The fire I built is still going. Nothing wrong. It works fine."

She was not satisfied.

That black stuff, she said. It didn't look well in a fireplace. She wanted it to look clean and unused; she was expecting a prospective tenant, and everything had to be satisfactory.

But he was an honorable man with no desire to cheat this woman.

"All fireplaces get black, Mrs. Hildegarde. It's the smoke. They all get that way. You can't help it."

No, it didn't look well.

He told her about muriatic acid. A solution of muriatic acid and water. Apply it with a brush: that would remove the blackness. Not more than two hours' work—

Two hours? That would never do. No, Mr. Bandini. She wanted all the firebrick taken out and new brick put in. He shook his head at the extravagance.

"That'll take a day and a half, Mrs. Hildegarde. Cost you twenty-five dollars, material included."

She pulled the coat around her, shivering in the cold room.

"Never mind the cost, Mr. Bandini," she said. "It has to be done. Nothing is too good for my tenants."

What could he say to that? Did Maria expect him to stalk off the job, refuse to do it? He acted like a sensible man, glad for this opportunity to make more money. The Widow drove him to the lumber yard.

It's so cold in that house," she said. "You should have some kind of a heater."

His answer was an artless confusion out of which he made it clear that if there is work there is warmth, that when a man has freedom of movement it is enough, for then his blood is hot too. But her concern left him hot and choking beside her in the car, her perfumed presence teasing him as his nostrils pulled steadily at the lush fragrance of her skin and garments. Her gloved hands swung the car to the curbing in front of the Gage Lumber Company.

Old Man Gage was standing at the window when Bandini got out and bowed goodby to the Widow. She crippled him with a relentless smile that shook his knees, but he was strutting like a defiant rooster when he stepped inside the office, slammed the door with an air of bravado, pulled out a cigar, scratched a match across the face of the counter, puffed the weed thoughtfully, blowing a burst of smoke into the face of Old Man Gage, who blinked his eyes and looked away after Bandini's brutal stare had penetrated his skull. Bandini grunted with satisfaction. Did he owe the Gage Lumber Company money ? Then let Old Man Gage take cognizance of the facts. Let him remember that with his own eyes he had seen Bandini among people of power. He gave the order for a hundred face brick, a sack of cement, and a yard of sand, to be delivered at the Windsor Street address.

"And hurry it up," he said over his shoulder. "I got to have it inside half an hour."

He swaggered back to the Windsor Street house, his chin in the air, the blue strong smoke from his Toscanelli tumbling over his shoulder. Maria should have seen the whipped dog expression on Old Man Gage's face, the obsequious alacrity with which he wrote down Bandini's order.

The materials were being delivered even as he arrived at the empty house, the Gage Lumber Co. truck backed against the front curb. Peeling off his coat, he plunged to the task. This, he vowed, would be one of the finest little bricklaying jobs in the state of Colorado. Fifty years from now, a hundred years from now, two hundred, the fireplace would still be standing. For when Svevo Bandini did a job, he did it well.

He sang as he worked, a song of Spring: *Come Back To Sorento*. The empty house sighed with echo, the cold rooms filling with the ring of his voice, the crack of his hammer and the plink of his trowel. Gala day: the time passed quickly. The room grew warm with the heat of his energy, the window panes wept for joy as the frost melted and the street became visible.

Now a truck drew up to the curb. Bandini paused in his work to watch the green-mackinawed driver lift a shining object and carry it toward the house. A red truck from the Watson Hardware Company. Bandini put down his trowel. He had made no delivery order with the Watson Hardware Company. No—he would never order anything from the Watson people. They had garnisheed his wages once for a bill he could not pay. He hated the Watson Hardware Company, one of his worst enemies.

"Your name Bandini?"

"What do you care?"

"I don't. Sign this."

An oil heater from Mrs. Hildegarde to Svevo Bandini. He signed the paper and the driver left. Bandini stood before the heater as though it was the Widow herself. He whistled in astonishment. This was too much for any man —too much.

"A fine woman," he said, shaking his head. "Very fine woman."

Suddenly there were tears in his eyes. The trowel fell from his hands as he dropped to his knees to examine the shining, nickel-plated heater. You're the finest woman in this town, Mrs. Hildegarde, and when I get through with this fireplace you'll be damn proud of it!"

Once more he returned to his work, now and then smiling at the heater over his shoulder, speaking to it as though it were his companion. "Hello there, Mrs. Hildegarde! You still there? Watching me, eh? Got your eye on Svevo Bandini, have you? Well, you're looking at the best bricklayer in Colorado, Lady."

The work advanced faster than he imagined. He carried on until it was too dark to see. By noon the next day he would be finished. He gathered his tools, washed his trowel, and prepared to leave. It was not until that late hour, standing in the murky light that came from the street lamp, that he realized he had forgotten to light the heater. His hands shrieked with cold. Setting the heater inside the fireplace, he lighted it and adjusted the flame to a dim glow. It was safe there: it could burn all night and prevent the fresh mortar from freezing.

He did not go home to his wife and children. He stayed with Rocco again that night. With Rocco, Maria; not with a woman, but with Rocco Saccone a man. And he slept well; no falling into black bottomless pits, no green-eyed serpents slithering after him through his dreams.

Maria might have asked why he didn't come home. That was his business. *Dio rospo!* Did he have to explain everything?

The next afternoon at four he was before the Widow with a bill for the work. He had written it on stationery from the Rocky Mountain Hotel. He was not a good speller and he knew it. He had simply put it this way: Work 40.00. And signed it. Half of that amount would go for materials. He had made twenty dollars. The Widow did not even look at the statement. She removed her reading glasses and insisted that he make himself at home. He thanked her for the heater. He was glad to be in her house. His joints were not so frozen as before. His feet had mastered the shining floor. He could anticipate the soft divan before he sat in it. The Widow depreciated the heater with a smile.

"That house was like an ice-box, Svevo."

Svevo. She had called him by his first name. He laughed outright. He had not meant to laugh, but the excitement of her mouth making his name got away from him. The blaze in the fireplace was hot. His wet shoes were close to it. Bitter smelling steam rose from them. The Widow was behind him, moving about; he dared not look. Once more he had lost the use of his voice. That icicle in his mouth

—that was his tongue: it would not move. That hot throbbing in his temples, making his hair seem on fire: that was the pounding of his brain: it would not give him words. The pretty Widow with two hundred thousand dollars in the bank had called him by his first name. The pine logs in the fire sputtered their sizzling mirth. He sat staring into the flame, his face set in a smile as he worked his big hands together, the bones cracking for joy. He did not move, transfixed with worry and delight, tormented by the loss of his voice. At last he was able to speak.

"Good fire," he said. "Good."

No answer. He looked over his shoulder. She was not there, but he heard her coming from the hall and he turned and fixed his bright excited eyes on the flame. She came with a tray bearing glasses and a bottle. She put it on the mantelpiece and poured two drinks. He saw the flash of diamonds on her fingers. He saw her solid hips, the streamline, the curve of her womanly back, the plump grace of her arm as she poured the liquor from the gurgling bottle.

"Here you are, Svevo. Do you mind if I call you that?"

He took the brownish red liquor and stared at it, wondering what it was, this drink the color of his eyes, this drink rich women put into their throats. Then he remembered that she had spoken to him about his name. His blood ran wild, bulging at the hot flushed limits of his face.

"I don't care, Mrs. Hildegarde, what you call me."

That made him laugh and he was happy that at last he had said something funny in the American style, even though he had not meant to do so. The liquor was Malaga, sweet, hot, powerful Spanish wine. He sipped it carefully, then tossed it away with vigorous peasant aplomb. It was sweet and hot in his stomach. He smacked his lips, pulled the big muscles of his forearm across his lips.

"By God, that's good."

She poured him another glassful. He made the conventional protests, his eyes popping with delight as the wine laughed its way into his outstretched glass.

"I have a surprise for you, Svevo."

She walked to the desk and returned with a package wrapped in Christmas paper. Her smile became a wince as she broke the red strings with her jeweled fingers and he watched in a suffocation of pleasure. She got it open and the tissue inside wrinkled as though little animals thrived in it. The gift was a pair of shoes. She held them out, a shoe in each hand, and watched the play of flame in his seething eyes. He could not bear it. His mouth formed a twist of incredulous torture, that she should know he needed shoes. He made grunts of protest, he swayed in the divan, he ran his gnarled fingers through his hair, he panted through a difficult smile, and then his eyes disappeared into a pool of tears. Again his forearm went up, streaked across his face, and pulled the wetness from his eyes. He fumbled through his pocket, produced a crackling red polka dot handkerchief, and cleared his nostrils with a rapid fire of snorts.

"You're being very silly, Svevo," she smiled. "I should think you'd be glad."

"No," he said. "No. Mrs. Hildegarde. I buy my own shoes."

He put his hand over his heart.

"You give me work, and I buy my own."

She swept it aside as absurd sentiment. The glass of wine offered distraction. He drained it, got up and filled it and drained it again. She came over to him and put her hand on his arm. He looked into her face that smile sympathetically, and once more a gusher of tears rose out of him and overflowed to his cheeks. Self-pity lashed him. That he should be subjected to such embarrassment! He sat down again, his fists clamped at his chin, his eyes closed. That this should happen to Svevo Bandini!

But, even as he wept he bent over to unlace his old soggy shoes. The right shoe came off with a sucking sound, exposing a grey sock with holes in the toes, the big toe red and naked. For some reason he wiggled it. The Widow laughed. Her amusement was his cure. His mortification vanished. Eagerly he went at the business of removing the other shoe. The Widow sipped wine and watched him.

The shoes were kangaroo, she told him, they were expensive. He pulled them on, felt their cool softness. God in heaven, what shoes! He laced them and stood up. He might have stepped barefoot into a deep carpet so soft they were, such friendly things at his feet. He walked across the room, trying them.

"Just right," he said. "Pretty good, Mrs. Hildegarde!"

What now? She turned her back and sat down. He walked to the fireplace.

"I'll pay you, Mrs. Hildegarde. What they cost you I'll take off the bill." It was inappropriate. Upon her face was an expectancy and a disappointment he could not fathom.

"The best shoes I ever had," he said, sitting down and stretching them before him. She threw herself at the opposite end of the divan. In a tired voice she asked him to pour her a drink. He gave it to her and she accepted it without thanks, saying nothing as she sipped the wine, sighing with faint exasperation. He sensed her uneasiness. Perhaps he had stayed too long. He got up to go. Vaguely he felt her smouldering silence. Her jaw was set, her lips a thin thread. Maybe she was sick, wanting to be alone. He picked up his old shoes and bundled them under his arm.

"I think maybe I'll go now, Mrs. Hildegarde."

She stared into the flames.

"Thank you Mrs. Hildegarde. If you have some more work sometime . . ."

"Of course, Svevo." She looked up and smiled. "You're a superb worker, Svevo. I'm well satisfied."

"Thank you, Mrs. Hildegarde."

What about his wages for the work? He crossed the room and hesitated at the door. She did not see him go. He took the knob in his hand and twisted it.

"Goodbye, Mrs. Hildegarde."

She sprang to her feet. Just a moment. There was something she had meant to ask him. That pile of stones in the back yard, left over from the house. Would he look at it before he went away? Perhaps he could tell her what to do with them. He followed the rounded hips through the hall to the back porch where he looked at the stones from the window, two tons of flagstone under snow. He thought a moment and made suggestions: she could do many things with that stone—lay down a sidewalk with it; build a low wall around the garden; erect a sundial and garden benches, a fountain, an incinerator. Her face was chalky and frightened as he turned from the window, his arm gently brushing her chin. She had been leaning over his shoulder, not quite touching it. He apologized. She smiled.

"We'll talk of it later," she said. "In the Spring."

She did not move, barring the path back to the hall.

"I want you to do all my work, Svevo."

Her eyes wandered over him. The new shoes attracted her. She smiled again. "How are they?"

"Best I ever had."

Still there was something else. Would he wait just a moment, until she thought of it? There was something —something—something—and she kept snapping her fingers and biting her lip thoughtfully. They went back through the narrow hallway. At the first door she stopped. Her hand fumbled at the knob. It was dim in the hall. She pushed the door open.

"This is my room," she said.

He saw the pounding of her heart in her throat. Her face was grey, her eyes bright with quick shame. Her jeweled hand covered the fluttering in her throat. Over her shoulder he saw the room, the white bed, the dressing table, the chest of drawers. She entered the room, switched on the light, and made a circle in the middle of the carpet.

"It's a pleasant room, don't you think?"

He watched her, not the room. He watched her, his eyes shifting to the bed and back to her again. He felt his mind warming, seeking the fruits of imagery; that woman and this room. She walked to the bed, her hips weaving like a cluster of serpents as she fell on the bed and lay there, her hand in an empty gesture.

"It's so pleasant here."

A wanton gesture, careless as wine. The fragrance of the place fed his heart-beat. Her eyes were feverish, her lips parted in an agonized expression that showed her teeth.

He could not be sure of himself. He squinted his eyes as he watched her. No—she could not mean it. This woman had too much money. Her wealth impeded the imagery. Such things did not happen.

She lay facing him, her head on her outstretched arm. The loose smile must have been painful, for it seemed to come with frightened uneasiness. His throat responded with a clamor of blood; he swallowed, and looked away, toward the door through the hall. What he had been thinking had best be forgotten. This woman was not interested in a poor man.

"I think I better go now, Mrs. Hildegarde."

"Fool," she smiled.

He grinned his confusion, the chaos of his blood and brain. The evening air would clear that up. He turned and walked down the hall to the front door.

"You fool!" he heard her say. "You ignorant peasant." *Mannaggia!* And she had not paid him, either. His lips screwed into a sneer. She could call Svevo Bandini a fool! She arose from the bed to meet him, her hands outstretched to embrace him. A moment later she was struggling to tear herself away. She winced in terrible joy as he stepped back, her ripped blouse streaming from his two fists.

He had torn her blouse away even as Maria had torn the flesh from his face. Remembering it now, that night in the Widow's bedroom was even yet worth a great deal to him.

No other living being was in that house, only himself and the woman against him, crying with ecstatic pain, weeping that he have mercy, her weeping a pretense, a beseechment for mercilessness. He laughed the triumph of his poverty and peasantry. This Widow! She with her wealth and deep plump warmth, slave and victim of her own challenge, sobbing in the joyful abandonment of her defeat, each gasp his victory. He could have done away with her had he desired, reduced her scream to a whisper, but he arose and walked into the room where the fireplace glowed lazily in the quick Winter darkness, leaving her weeping and choking on the bed. Then she came to him there at the fireplace and fell on her knees before him, her face sodden with tears, and he smiled and lent himself once more to her delicious torment. And when he left her sobbing in her fulfillment, he walked down the road with deep content that came from the conviction he was master of the earth.

So be it. Tell Maria? This was the business of his own soul. Not telling, he had done Maria a favor—she with her rosaries and prayers, her commandments and indulgences. Had she asked, he would have lied. But she had not asked. Like a cat she had leaped to the conclusions written on his lacerated face. Thou shalt not commit adultery. Bah. It was the Widow's doing. He was her victim.

She had committed adultery. A willing victim.

Every day he was at her house during the Christmas week. Sometimes he whistled as he sounded the foxhead knocker. Sometimes he was silent. Always the door swung open after a moment and a welcome smile met his eyes. He could not shake loose from his embarrassment. Always that house was a place where he did not belong, exciting and unattainable. She greeted him in blue dresses and red dresses, yellow and green. She bought him cigars, Chancellors in a Christmas box. They were on the mantelpiece before his eyes; he knew they were his but he always waited for her invitation to take one.

A strange rendezvous. No kisses and no embraces. She would take his hand as he entered and shake it warmly. She was so glad he had come—wouldn't he like to sit down for awhile? He thanked her and crossed the room to the fireplace. A few words about the weather; a polite enquiry about his health. Silence as she returned to her book.

Five minutes, ten.

No sound save the swish of book pages. She would look up and smile. He always sat with his elbows on his knees, his thick neck bloated, staring at the flames, thinking his own thoughts: of his home, his children, of the woman beside him, of her wealth, wondering about her past. The swish of pages, the clucking and hissing of pine logs. Then she would look up again. Why didn't he smoke a cigar?

They were his; help yourself. Thank you, Mrs. Hildegarde. And he would light up, pulling at the fragrant leaf, watching the white smoke tumble from his cheeks, thinking his own thoughts.

In the decanter on the low table was whiskey, with glasses and soda beside it. Did he desire a drink? Then he would wait, the minutes passing, the pages swishing, until she glanced at him once more, her smile a courtesy to let him know she remembered he was there.

"Won't you have a drink, Svevo?"

Protests, the moving about in his chair, flicking away his cigar ash, jerking at his collar. No thank you, Mrs. Hildegarde: he was not what you'd call a drinking man. Once in awhile—yes. But not today. She listened with that parlor smile, peering at him over her reading glasses, not really listening at all.

"If you feel that you'd like one, don't hesitate."

Then he poured a tumblerful, disposing of it with a professional jerk. His stomach took it like ether, blotting it away and creating the desire for more. The ice was broken. He poured another and another; expensive whiskey out of a bottle from Scotland, forty cents a shot down at the Imperial Poolhall. But there was always some little prelude of uneasiness, a whistling in the dark, before he poured one; a cough, or he might rub his hands together and stand up to let her know he was about to drink again, or the humming of a shapeless nameless tune. After that it was easier, the liquor freeing him, and he tossed them down without hesitancy. The whiskey, like the cigars, was for him. When he left, the decanter was emptied and when he returned it was full again.

It was ever the same, a waiting for evening shadows, the Widow reading and he smoking and drinking. It could not last. Christmas Eve, and it would be over. There was something about that time and season—Christmas coming, the old year dying—that told him it would be for only a few days, and he felt that she knew it, too.

Down the hill and at the other end of town was his family, his wife and children. Christmas time was the time for wife and children. He would leave, never to return. In his pockets would be money. Meantime, he liked it here. He liked the fine whiskey, the fragrant cigars. He liked this pleasant room and the rich woman who lived in it. She was not far from him, reading her book, and in a little while she would walk into the bedroom and he would follow. She would gasp and weep and then he would leave in the twilight, triumph giving zest to his legs. The leave-taking he loved most of all. That surge of satisfaction, that vague chauvinism telling him no people on earth equalled the Italian people, that joy in his peasantry. The Widow had money—yes. But back there she lay, crushed, and Bandini was a better man than she, by God.

He might have gone home those nights had there been that feeling that it was over. But it was no time for thinking of his family. A few days more and his worries would begin again. Let those days be spent in a world apart from his own. No one knew save his friend Rocco Saccone.

Rocco was happy for him, lending him shirts and ties, throwing open his big wardrobe of suits. Lying in the darkness before sleep, he would wait for Bandini's account of that day. Concerning other matters, they spoke in English, but of the Widow it was always in Italian, whispered and secretive.

"She wants to marry me," Bandini would say. "She was on her knees, begging me to divorce Maria."

"*Si,*" Rocco answered. "Indeed!"

"Not only that, but she promised to settle a hundred thousand dollars on me."

"And what did you say?"

"I am considering it," he lied.

Rocco gasped, swung around in the darkness.

"Considering it! *Sangue de la madonna!* Have you lost your mind? Take it! Take fifty thousand! Ten thousand! Take anything—do it for nothing!"

No, Bandini told him, the proposition was out of the question. A hundred thousand would certainly go a long way toward solving his problems, but Rocco seemed to forget that there was a question of honor here, and Bandini had no desire to dishonor his wife and children for mere gold. Rocco groaned and tore his hair, muttering curses.

"Jackass!" he said. "Ah *Dio!* What a jackass!"

It shocked Bandini. Did Rocco mean to tell him that he would actually sell his honor for money—for a hundred thousand dollars? Exasperated, Rocco snapped the light switch above the bed. Then he sat up, his face livid, his eyes protruding, his red fists clinching the collar of his winter underwear. "You wish to know if I would sell my honor for a hundred thousand dollars?" he demanded. "Then look here!" With that he gave his arm a jerk, tearing open his underwear in front, the buttons flying and scattering over the floor. He sat pounding his naked chest savagely over his heart. "I would not only sell my honor," he shouted. "I would sell myself body and soul, for at least fifteen hundred dollars!"

There was the night when Rocco asked Bandini to introduce him to the Widow Hildegarde. Bandini shook his head doubtfully. "You would not understand her, Rocco. She is a woman of great learning, a college graduate."

"Pooh!" Rocco said indignantly. "Who the hell are you?"

Bandini pointed out that the Widow Hildegarde was a constant reader of books, whereas Rocco could neither read nor write in English. Furthermore, Rocco still spoke English poorly. His presence would only do harm to the rest of the Italian people.

Rocco sneered. "What of that ?" he said. "There are other things besides reading and writing." He crossed the room to the clothes closet and flung open the door. "Reading and writing !" he sneered. "And what good has it done you ? Do you have as many suits of clothes as I ? As many neckties ? I have more clothes than the president of the University of Colorado—what good have reading and writing done him ?"

He smiled that Rocco should reason thus, but Rocco had the right idea. Bricklayers and college presidents, they were all the same. A matter of where and why.

"I will speak to the Widow on your behalf," he promised. "But she is not interested in what a man wears. *Dio cane,* it is just the other way around."

Rocco nodded sagely.

"Then I have nothing to worry about."

His last hours with the Widow were like the first. Hello and goodbye, they added up to the same thing. They were strangers, with passion alone to bridge the chasm of their differences, and there was no passion that afternoon.

"My friend Rocco Saccone," Bandini said. "He's a good bricklayer too."

She lowered her book and looked at him over the rim of her gold reading glasses.

"Indeed," she murmured.

He twirled his whiskey glass.

"He's a good man, all right."

"Indeed," she said again. For some minutes she continued to read. Perhaps he should not have said that. The obvious implication startled him.

He sat laboring in the muddle he had made of it, the sweat breaking out, an absurd grin plastered across the sickly convolutions of his face. More silence. He looked out the window. Already the night was at work, rolling shadowy carpets across the snow. Soon it would be time to go.

It was bitterly disappointing. If only something beside the beast stalked between himself and this woman. If he could but tear away that curtain the fact of her wealth spread before him. Then he might talk as he did to any woman. She made him so stupid. *Jesu Christi!* He was no fool. He could talk. He had a mind which reasoned and fought through hardships far greater than hers. Of books, no. There had been no time in his driven, worried life for books. But he had read deeper into the language of life than she, despite her ubiquitous books. He brimmed with a world of things to speak about.

As he sat there, staring at her for what he believed to be the last time, he realized that he was not afraid of this woman. That he had never been afraid of her, that it was she who feared him. The truth angered him, his mind shuddering at the prostitution to which he had subjected his flesh. She did not look up from her book. She did not see the brooding insolence twisting one side of his face. Suddenly he was glad it was the end. With an unhurried swagger he rose and crossed to the window.

"Getting dark," he said. "Pretty soon I'll go away and won't come back no more."

The book came down automatically.

"Did you say something, Svevo?"

"Pretty soon I won't come back no more."

"It *has* been delightful, hasn't it?"

"You don't understand nothing," he said. "Nothing."

"What do you mean?"

He did not know. It was there, yet not there. He opened his mouth to speak, opened his hands and spread them out.

"A woman like you . . ."

He could say no more. If he succeeded, it would be crude and badly phrased, defeating the thing he wanted to explain. He shrugged futilely.

Let it go, Bandini; forget it.

She was glad to see him sit down again, smiling her satisfaction and returning to her book. He looked at her bitterly. This woman—she did not belong to the race of human beings. She was so cold, a parasite upon his vitality. He resented her politeness: it was a lie. He despised her complacency, he loathed her good breeding. Surely, now that it was over and he was going away, she could put down that book and talk to him. Perhaps they would say nothing important, but he was willing to try, and she was not.

"I musn't forget to pay you," she said.

A hundred dollars. He counted it, shoved it into his back pocket.

"Is it enough?" she asked.

He smiled; "If I did not need this money a million dollars would not be enough."

"Then you want more. Two hundred?"

Better not to quarrel. Better to leave and be gone forever, without bitterness. He pushed his fists through his coat sleeves and chewed the end of his cigar.

"You'll come to see me, won't you?"

"To be sure, Mrs. Hildegarde."

But he was certain he would never return.

"Good-bye, Mr. Bandini."

"Good-bye, Mrs. Hildegarde."

"A merry Christmas."

"The same to you, Mrs. Hildegarde."

Good-bye and hello again in less than an hour.

The Widow opened the door to his knocking and saw the dotted handkerchief masking all but his bloodshot eyes. Her breath shot back in horror.

"God in heaven!"

He stamped the snow from his feet and brushed the front of his coat with one hand. She could not see the bitter pleasure in the smile behind the handkerchief, nor hear the muffled Italian curses. Someone was to blame for this, and it was not Svevo Bandini. His eyes accused her as he stepped inside, snow from his shoes melting in a pool on the carpet.

She retreated to the bookcase, watching him speechlessly. The heat from the fireplace stung his face. With a groan of rage he hurried to the bathroom. She followed, standing at the open door as he blubbered into fistfuls of cold water. Her cheeks crept with pity as he gasped. When he looked into the mirror he saw the twisted, torn image of himself and it repulsed him, and he shook his head in a rage of denial.

"Ah, poor Svevo!"

What was it? What had happened?

"What do you suppose?"

"Your wife?"

He dabbed the cuts with salve.

"But this is impossible!"

"Bah."

She stiffened, lifting her chin proudly.

"I tell you it's impossible. Who could have told her?"

"How do I know who told her?"

He found a bandage kit in the cabinet and began tearing

strips of gauze and adhesive. The tape was tough. He shrieked a volley of curses at its obstinacy, breaking it against his knee with a violence that staggered him backward toward the bathtub. In triumph he held the strip of tape before his eyes and leered at it.

"Don't get tough with *me!*" he said to the tape.

Her hand was raised to help him.

"No," he growled. "No piece of tape can get the best of Svevo Bandini."

She turned away. When she came back he was applying gauze and tape. There were four long strips on either cheek, reaching from his eyeballs to his chin. He saw her and was startled. She was dressed to go out: fur coat, blue scarf, hat, and galoshes. That quiet elegance of her appeal, that rich simplicity of her tiny hat tipped jauntily to the side, the bright wool scarf spilling from the luxurious collar of her fur, the grey galoshes with their neat buckles and the long grey driving gloves, stamped her again for what she was, a rich woman subtly proclaiming her difference. He was awed.

"The door at the end of the hall is an extra bedroom," she said. "I should be back around midnight."

"You're going someplace?"

"It's Christmas Eve." She said it as though, had it been any other day, she would have stayed home.

She was gone, the sound of her car drifting to nothing

down the mountain road. Now a strange impulse seized him. He was alone in the house, all alone. He walked to her room and groped and searched through her effects. He opened drawers, examined old letters and papers. At the dressing table he lifted the cork from every perfume bottle, sniffed it, and returned it exactly to where he had found it. Here was a desire he had long felt, bursting out of control now that he was alone, this desire to touch and smell and fondle and examine at leisure everything that was her possession. He caressed her lingerie, pressed her cold jewels between his palms. He opened inviting little drawers in her writing desk, studied the fountain pens and pencils, the bottles and boxes therein. He peered into shelves, searched through trunks, removing each item of apparel, every nicknack and jewel and souvenir, studied each with care, evaluated it, and returned it to the place whence it had come. Was he a thief groping for plunder? Did he seek the mystery of this woman's past? No and no again. Here was a new world and he wished to know it well. That and no more.

It was after eleven when he sank into the deep bed in the extra room. Here was a bed the like of which his bones had never known. It seemed that he sank miles before dropping to sweet rest. Around his ears the satin eiderdown blankets pressed their gentle warm weight. He sighed with something like a sob. This night at least, there would be peace. He lay talking to himself softly in the language of his nativity.

"All will be well—a few days and all will be forgotten. She needs me. My children need me. A few more days and she will get over it."

From afar he heard the tolling of bells, the call for midnight mass at the Church of the Sacred Heart. He rose to one elbow and listened. Christmas morning. He saw his wife kneeling at mass, his three sons in pious procession down the main altar as the choir sang *Adeste Fideles.* His wife, his pitiful Maria. Tonight she would be wearing that battered old hat, as old as their marriage, remade year after year to meet as far as possible the new styles. Tonight—nay, at that very moment—he knew she knelt on wearied knees, her trembling lips moving in prayer for himself and his children. Oh star of Bethlehem! Oh birth of the Infant Jesus!

Through the window he saw the tumbling flakes of snow, Svevo Bandini in another woman's bed as his wife prayed for his immortal soul. He lay back, sucking the big tears that streamed down his bandaged face. Tomorrow he would go home again. It had to be done. On his knees he would sue for forgiveness and peace. On his knees, after the kids were gone and his wife was alone. He could never do it in their presence. The kids would laugh and spoil it all.

One glance at the mirror next morning killed his determination. There was the hideous image of his ravaged face, now purple and swollen, black puffs under the eyes. He could meet no man with those telltale scars. His own sons would flinch in horror. Growling and cursing, he threw himself into a chair and tore at his hair. *Jesu Christi!* He dared not even walk the streets. No man, seeing him, could fail to read the language of violence scrawled upon his countenance. For all the lies he might tell—that he had fallen on the ice, that he had fought a man over a card game—there could be no doubt that a woman's hands had torn his cheeks.

He dressed, and tiptoed past the Widow's closed door to the kitchen, where he ate a breakfast of bread and butter and black coffee. After washing the dishes he returned to his room. Out of the corner of his eye he caught sight of himself on the dresser mirror. The reflection angered him so that he clinched his fists, and controlled the desire to smash the mirror. Moaning and cursing, he threw himself on the bed, his head rolling from side to side as he realized it might be a week before the scratches would heal and the swelling subside so that his face was fit for the gaze of human society.

A sunless Christmas day. The snowing had stopped. He lay listening to the patter of melting icicles. Toward noon he heard the cautious knocking of the Widow's knuckles on the door. He knew it was she, yet he leaped out of bed like a criminal pursued by the police.

"Are you there?" she asked.

He could not face her.

"One moment!" he said.

Quickly he opened the top dresser drawer, whipped out a hand towel, and bound it over his face, masking all but his eyes. Then he opened the door. If she was startled by his appearance, she did not show it. Her hair was pulled up in a thin net, her plump figure wrapped in a frilled pink dressing gown.

"Merry Christmas," she smiled.

"My face," he apologized, pointing to it. "The towel keeps it warm. Makes it get well quick."

"Did you sleep well?"

"Best bed I ever slept in. Fine bed, very soft."

She crossed the room and sat on the edge of the bed, bouncing herself experimentally. "Why," she said, "It's softer than mine."

"Pretty good bed, all right."

She hesitated, then stood up. Her eyes met his frankly.

"You know you're welcome," she said. "I hope you'll stay."

What should he say? He stood in silence, his mind searching about until he came upon a suitable reply. "I'll pay you board and room," he said. "Whatever you charge, I'll pay."

"Why, the idea!" she answered. "Don't you dare suggest such a thing! You're my guest. This is no boarding house—this is my home!"

"You're a good woman, Mrs. Hildegarde. Fine woman."

"Nonsense!"

Just the same, he made up his mind to pay her. Two or three days, until his face healed . . . Two dollars a day . . . No more of the other thing.

There was something else:

"We'll have to be very careful," she said. "You know how people talk."

"I know, all right," he answered.

Still there was something more. She dug her fingers into the pocket of the dressing gown. A key with a beaded chain attached.

"It's for the side door," she said.

She dropped it into his open palm and he examined it, pretending it was a most extraordinary thing, but it was only a key and after awhile he shoved it into his pocket.

One more matter:

She hoped he didn't mind, but this was Christmas Day, this afternoon she expected guests. Christmas gifts and such things.

"So perhaps it would be best."

"Sure," he interrupted. "I know."

"There's no great hurry. An hour or so."

Then she left. Pulling the towel from his face, he sat on the bed and rubbed the back of his neck in bewilderment. Again his glance caught the hideous image in the mirror. *Dio Christo!* If anything, he looked even worse. What was he to do now?

Suddenly he saw himself in another light. The stupidity of his position revolted him. What manner of jackass was he, that he could be led away by the nose because people were coming to this house? He was no criminal; he was a man, a good man too. He had a trade. He belonged to the union. He was an American citizen. He was a father, with sons. Not far away was his home; perhaps it did not belong to him, but it was his home, a roof of his own. What had come over him, that he should skulk and hide like a murderer? He had done wrong—*certamente*—but where upon the earth was a man who hadn't?

His face—bah!

He stood before the mirror and sneered. One by one he peeled off the bandages. There were other things more important than his face. Besides, in a few days it would be as good as new. He was no coward; he was Svevo Bandini; above all, a man—a brave man. Like a man he would stand before Maria and ask her to forgive him. Not to beg. Not to plead. Forgive me, he would say. Forgive me. I done wrong. It won't happen again.

The determination sent a chill of satisfaction through

him. He grabbed his coat, pulled his hat down over his eyes, and walked quietly out of the house without a word to the Widow.

Christmas Day! He threw his chest into it, dragged deep breaths of it down. What a Christmas this would be! How fine to bear out the courage of his convictions. The splendor of being a brave and an honorable man! Reaching the first street within the city limits, he saw a woman in a red hat approaching him. Here was the test for his face. He threw back his shoulders, tilted his chin. To his delight, the woman did not even look at him after her first quick glance. The rest of the way home, he whistled *Adeste Fideles*.

Maria, here I come!

The snow in the front walk had not been shoveled. Ho, and so the kids were loafing on the job during his absence. Well, he would put a stop to that immediately. From now on, things would be run differently. Not only himself, but the whole family would turn over a new leaf, beginning this day.

Strange, but the front door was locked, the curtains pulled down. Not so strange at that: he remembered that on Christmas Day there were five masses at the church, the last mass at twelve noon. The boys would be there. Maria, however, always went to midnight mass on Christmas Eve. Then she must be home. He pounded the screen without success. Then he went around to the back door and it was locked too. He peered into the kitchen window. A funnel of steam coming from the tea-kettle on the stove told him that someone was certainly there. He pounded again, this time with both fists. No answer.

"What the devil," he grumbled, continuing around the house to the window of his own bedroom. Here the shades were down, but the window was open. He scratched it with his nails, calling her name.

"Maria. Oh, Maria."

"Who is it ?" The voice was sleepy, tired.

"It's me, Maria. Open up."

"What do you want ?"

He heard her rising from bed and the movement of a chair, as though bumped in the darkness. The curtain opened from the side and he saw her face, thick with sleep, her eyes uncertain and retreating from the blinding white snow. He choked, laughed a little in joy and fear.

"Maria."

"Go away," she said. "I don't want you."

The curtain closed again.

"But Maria. Listen !"

Her voice was tense, excited.

"I don't want you near me. Go away. I can't stand the sight of you !"

He pressed the screen with the palms of his hand and laid his head against it, beseeching her. "Maria, please. I have something to say to you. Open the door Maria, let me talk."

"Oh God!" she screamed. "Get away, get away! I hate you, I hate you!" Then there was a crash of something through the green curtain, a flash as he jerked his head aside, and the harsh tearing of screen-wire so close to his ear that he felt he had been struck. From within he heard her sobbing and choking. He drew back and examined the broken curtain and screen. Buried in the screen, pierced through to the handle, was a long pair of sewing scissors. He was sweating in every pore as he walked back to the street, and his heart was working like a sledge-hammer. Reaching into his pocket for a handkerchief, his fingers touched something cold and metallic. It was the key the Widow had given him.

Good, then. So be it.

9.

CHRISTMAS VACATION WAS OVER, AND ON January 6th school reopened. It had been a disastrous vacation, ever unhappy and full of strife. Two hours before the first bell August and Federico sat on the front steps of St. Catherine's, waiting for the janitor to open the door. It wasn't a good idea to go around saying it openly, but school was a lot better than home.

Not so with Arturo.

Anything was better than facing Rosa again. He left home a few minutes before class, walking slowly, preferring to be late and avoiding any chance meeting with her in the hall. He arrived fifteen minutes after bell-time, dragging himself up the stairs as though his legs were broken. His manner changed the moment his hand touched the doorknob of the classroom. Brisk and alert, panting as though after a hard run, he turned the knob, whisked inside, and tiptoed hurriedly to his seat.

Sister Mary Celia was at the blackboard, at the opposite side of the room from Rosa's desk. He was glad, for it spared him any stray encounter with Rosa's soft eyes. Sister Celia was explaining the square of a right triangle, and with some violence, bits of chalk spattering as she lashed the blackboard with big defiant figures, her glass eye brighter than ever as it shot in his direction and back to the blackboard. He recalled the rumor among the kids about the eye: that when she slept at night, the eye glowed on her dresser, staring intently, becoming more luminous if burglars were about. She finished at the blackboard, slapping her hands clean of chalk.

"Bandini," she said. "You've begun the new year true to form. An explanation please."

He stood up.

"This is going to be good," someone whispered.

I went over to the church and said the rosary," Arturo said. "I wanted to offer up the new year to the Blessed Virgin."

That was always incontestible.

"Boloney," someone whispered.

"I want to believe you," Sister Celia said. "Even though I can't. Sit down."

He bent to his seat, shielding the left side of his face with his cupped hands. The geometry discussion droned on. He opened his text and spread it out, both hands hiding his face. But he had to have one look at her. Opening his fingers, he peeked through. Then he sat erect.

Rosa's desk was empty. He swung his head around the room. She was not there. Rosa wasn't in school. For ten minutes he tried to be relieved and glad. Then he saw blondie Gertie Williams across the aisle. Gertie and Rosa were friends.

Psssssssst, Gertie.

She looked at him.

"Hey Gertie, where's Rosa?"

"She isn't here."

"I know that, stupid. Where is she?"

"I don't know. Home, I guess."

He hated Gertie. He had always hated her and that pale pointed jaw of hers, always moving with chewing gum. Gertie always got B's, thanks to Rosa who helped her. But Gertie was so transparent, you could almost see through her white eyes to the back of her head, where there was nothing, nothing at all except her hunger for boys, and not a boy like himself, because he was the kind with dirty nails, because Gertie had that aloof air of making him feel her dislike.

"Have you seen her lately?"

"Not lately."

"When did you see her last?"

"Quite awhile ago."

"When ? You lunkhead !"

"New Year's Day," Gertie smiled superciliously.

"Is she quitting here ? Is she going to another school ?"

"I don't think so."

"How can you be so dumb ?'

"Don't you like it ?"

"What do *you* think ?"

"Then please don't talk to me, Arturo Bandini, because I certainly don't want to talk to you."

Nuts. His day was ruined. All these years he and Rosa had been in the same class. Two of those years he had been in love with her; day after day, seven and a half years of Rosa in the same room with him, and now her desk was empty. The only thing on earth he cared for, next to baseball, and she was gone, only thin air around the place that once blossomed with her black hair. That and a little red desk with a film of dust upon it.

Sister Mary Celia's voice became rasping and impossible. The geometry lesson faded into English composition. He pulled out his Spalding Yearbook of Organized Baseball and studied the batting and fielding averages of Wally Ames, third baseman for the Toledo Mudhens, up in the American Association.

Agnes Hobson, that phony little applepolishing screwball with the crooked front teeth spliced with copper wire, was reading aloud from Sir Walter Scott's *Lady of the Lake.*

Fooey, what bunk. To fight off boredom, he figured the life-time career average of Wally Ames and compared it with that of Nick Cullop, mighty fencebuster with the Atlanta Crackers way down there in the Southern Association. Cullop's average, after an hour of intricate mathematics spread over five sheets of paper, was ten points higher than Wally Ames'.

He sighed with pleasure. There was something about that name—Nick Cullop—a thump and a wallop about it, that pleased him more than the prosaic Wally Ames. He ended with a hatred of Ames and fell to musing about Cullop, what he looked like, what he talked about, what he would do if Arturo asked him in a letter for his autograph. The day was exhausting. His thighs ached and his eyes watered sleepily. He yawned and sneered without discrimination at everything Sister Celia discussed. He spent the afternoon bitterly regretting the things he had not done, the temptations he had resisted, during the vacation period which was passed now and gone forever.

The deep days, the sad days.

He was on time the next morning, pacing his approach to the school to coincide with the bell just as his feet crossed the front threshold. He hurried up the stairs and was looking toward Rosa's desk before he could see it through the cloak room wall. The desk was empty. Sister Mary Celia called the roll.

Payne. Present.

Penigle. Present.

Pinelli.

Silence.

He watched the nun inscribe an X in the roll book. She slipped the book in the desk drawer and called the class to order for morning prayers. The ordeal had begun again.

"Take out your geometry texts."

Go jump in the lake, he thought.

Pssssssst. Gertie.

"Seen Rosa ?"

"No."

"Is she in town ?"

"I don't know."

"She's your friend. Why don't you find out ?"

"Maybe I will. And maybe I won't."

"Nice girl."

"Don't cha like it ?"

"I'd like to punch that gum down your throat."

"Wouldn't you, though !"

At noon he strolled to the baseball diamond. Since Christmas no snow had fallen. The sun was furious, yellow with rage in the sky, avenging himself upon a mountain world that had slept and frozen in his absence. Dabs of snow tumbled from the naked cottonwoods around the ball field, falling to the ground and surviving for yet a moment as that yellow mouth in the sky lapped them into oblivion. Steam oozed from the earth, misty stuff oozing out of the earth and slinking away. In the West the storm clouds galloped off in riotous retreat, leaving off their attack on the mountains, the huge innocent peaks lifting their pointed lips thankfully toward the sun.

A warm day, but too wet for baseball. His feet sank in the sighing black mud around pitcher's box. Tomorrow, perhaps. Or the next day. But where was Rosa ? He leaned against one of the cottonwoods. This was Rosa's land. This was Rosa's tree. Because you've looked at it, because maybe you've touched it. And those are Rosa's mountains, and maybe she's looking at them now. Whatever she looked upon was hers, and whatever he looked upon was hers.

He passed her house after school, walking on the opposite side of the street. Cut Plug Wiggins, who delivered the Denver *Post*, moved by on his bike, nonchalantly flipping evening papers on every front porch. Arturo whistled and caught up with him.

"You know Rosa Pinelli ?"

Cut Plug spewed a gusher of tobacco juice across the snow. "You mean that Eyetalian dame three houses down the street ? Sure, I know her, why ?"

"Seen her lately ?"

"Nah."

"When did you see her last, Cut Plug ?"

Cut Plug leaned over the handlebars, wiped sweat from his face, spewed tobacco juice again, and lapsed into a careful checkup. Arturo stood by patiently, hoping for good news.

"The last time I seen her was three years ago," Cut Plug said at last. "Why?"

"Nothing," he said. "Forget it."

Three years ago! And the fool had said it as though it didn't matter.

The deep days, the sad days.

Home was chaos. Arriving from school, they found the doors open, the cold evening air in possession. The stoves were dead, their bins spilling ashes. Where is she? And they searched. She was never far away, sometimes down in the pasture in the old stone barn, seated on a box or leaning against the wall, her lips moving. Once they looked for her until long after dark, covering the neighborhood, peeking into barns and sheds, seeking her footsteps along the banks of the little creek that had grown overnight to a brownish, blasphemous bully, eating the earth and the trees as it roared defiance. They stood on the bank and watched the snarling current. They did not speak. They scattered and searched upstream and down. An hour later they returned to the house. Arturo built the fire. August and Federico huddled over it.

"She'll be home pretty soon."

"Sure."

"Maybe she went to church."

"Maybe."

Beneath their feet they heard her. There they found her, down in the cellar, kneeling over that barrel of wine Papa had vowed not to open until it was ten years old. She paid no attention to their entreaties. She looked coldly at August's tear-swept eyes. They knew they did not matter. Arturo took her arm gently, to raise her up. Quickly the back of her hand slapped him across the face. Silly. He laughed, a bit self-conscious, standing with his hand touching his red cheek.

"Leave her alone," he told them. "She wants to be alone."

He ordered Federico to get her a blanket. He pulled one from the bed and came down with it, stepping up and dropping it over her shoulders. She raised herself up, the blanket slipping away and covering her legs and feet. There was nothing more to do. They went upstairs and waited.

A long time afterward she appeared. They were around the kitchen table, fooling with their books, trying to be industrious, trying to be good boys. They saw her purple lips. They heard her grey voice.

"Have you had supper?"

Sure, they had supper. A swell supper too. They cooked it themselves.

"What did you have?"

They were afraid to answer.

Until Arturo spoke up: "Bread and butter."

"There isn't any butter," she said. "There hasn't been any butter in this house for three weeks."

That made Federico cry.

She was asleep in the morning when they left for school. August wanted to go in and kiss her goodbye. So did Federico. They wanted to say something about their lunches, but she was asleep, that strange woman on the bed who didn't like them.

"Better leave her alone."

They sighed and walked away. To school. August and Federico together, and in a little while Arturo, after lowering the fire and taking a last look around. Should he waken her? No, let her sleep. He filled a glass of water and put it at the bedside. Then to school, tiptoeing away.

Psssssst. Gertie.

"What do you want?"

"Seen Rosa?"

"No."

"What's happening to her, anyway?"

"I don't know."

"Is she sick?"

"I don't think so."

"You *can't* think. You're too dumb."

"Then don't talk to me."

At noon he walked out to the field again. The sun was still angry. The mound around the infield had dried, and most of the snow was gone. There was one spot against the right field fence in the shadows where the wind had banked the snow and thrown a dirty lace over it. But it was dry enough otherwise, perfect weather for practice. He spent the rest of the noon hour sounding out the members of the team. How about a workout tonight?—the ground's perfect. They listened to him with strange faces, even Rodriquez, the catcher, the one kid in all the school who loved baseball as fanatically as himself. Wait, they told him. Wait until Spring, Bandini. He argued with them about it. He won the argument. But after school, after sitting alone for an hour under the cottonwoods bordering the field, he knew they would not come, and he walked home slowly, past Rosa's house, on the same side of the street, right up to Rosa's front lawn. The grass was so green and bright he could taste it in his mouth. A woman came out of the house next door, got her paper, scanned the headlines, and stared at him suspiciously. I'm not doing anything: I'm just passing by. Whistling a hymn, he walked on down the street.

The deep days, the sad days.

His mother had done the washing that day. He arrived home through the alley and saw it hanging on the line. It had grown dark and suddenly cold. The washing hung stiff and frozen. He touched each stiffened garment as he walked up the path, brushing his hand against them to the end of the line. A queer time to wash clothes, for Monday had always been wash day. Today was Wednesday, maybe Thursday; certainly it was not Monday. A queer washing too. He stopped on the back porch to unravel the queerness. Then he saw what it was: every garment hanging there, clean and stiff, belonged to his father. Nothing of his own or his brothers, not even a pair of socks.

Chicken for dinner. He stood in the door and reeled as the fragrance of roast chicken filled his nostrils. Chicken, but how come? The only fowl left in the pen was Tony, the big rooster. His mother would never kill Tony. His mother loved that Tony with his jaunty thick comb and his fine strutting plumes. She had put red celluloid anklets on his spurred legs and laughed at his mighty swagger. But Tony it was: on the drainboard he saw the anklets broken in half like two red fingernails.

In a little while they tore him to pieces, tough though he was. But Maria did not touch him. She sat dipping bread into a yellow film of olive oil spread across her plate. Reminiscences of Tony: what a rooster he had been! They mused over his long reign in the chicken yard: they remembered him *when*. Maria dipped her bread in olive oil and stared.

"Something happens but you can't tell," she said. "Because if you have faith in God you have to pray, but I don't go around saying it."

Their jaws ceased and they looked at her.

Silence.

"What'd you say, Mamma?"

"I didn't say a word."

Federico and August glanced at one another and tried to smile. Then August's face turned white and he got up and left the table. Federico grabbed a piece of white meat and followed. Arturo put his fists under the table and squeezed them until the pain in his palms drove back the desire to cry.

"What chicken!" he said. "You ought to try it, Mamma. Just a taste."

"No matter what happens, you have to have faith," she said. "I don't have fine dresses and I don't go to dances with him, but I have faith, and they don't know it. But God knows it, and the Virgin Mary, and no matter what happens they know it. Sometimes I sit here all day, and no matter what happens they know because God died on the cross."

"Sure they know it," he said.

He got up and put his arms around her and kissed her. He saw into her bosom: the white drooping breasts, and he thought of little children, of Federico in infancy.

"Sure they know it," he said again. But he felt it coming

from his toes, and he could not bear it. "Sure they know it, Mamma."

He threw back his shoulders and strolled out of the kitchen to the clothes closet in his own room. He took the half-filled laundry bag from the hook behind the door and crushed it around his face and mouth. Then he let it go, howling and crying until his sides ached. When he was finished, dry and clean inside, no pain except the sting in his eyes as he stepped into the living room light, he knew that he had to find his father.

"Watch her," he said to his brothers. She had gone back to bed and they could see her through the open door, her face turned away.

"What'll we do if she does something?" August said.

"She won't do anything. Be quiet, and nice."

Moonlight. Bright enough to play ball. He took the shortcut across the trestle bridge. Below him, under the bridge, transients huddled over a red and yellow fire. At midnight they would grab the fast freight for Denver, thirty miles away. He found himself scanning the faces, seeking that of his father. But Bandini would not be down there; the place to find his father was at the Imperial Poolhall, or up in Rocco Saccone's room. His father belonged to the Union. He wouldn't be down there.

Nor was he in the cardroom at the Imperial.

Jim the bartender.

"He left about two hours ago with that Wop stonecutter."

"You mean Rocco Saccone?"

"That's him—that goodlooking Eyetalian."

He found Rocco in his room, seated at a table radio by the window, eating walnuts and listening to the jazz come out. A newspaper was spread at his feet to catch the walnut shells. He stood at the door, the soft darkness of Rocco's eyes letting him know he was not welcome. But his father was not in the room, not a sign of him.

"Where's my father, Rocco?"

"How do I know? He'sa your fodder. He'sa not my fodder."

But he had a boy's instinct for the truth.

"I thought he was living here with you."

"He'sa live by hisself."

Arturo checked it: a lie.

"Where does he live, Rocco?"

Rocco tossed his hands.

"I canna' say. I no see him no more."

Another lie.

"Jim the bartender says you were with him tonight."

Rocco jumped to his feet and waved his fist.

"That Jeem, she'sa lyin' bastard! He'sa come along stick hissa' nose where she'sa got no business. You fodder, he'sa man. He know what he'sa doing."

Now he knew.

"Rocco," he said. "Do you know a woman, Effie Hilde-garde ?"

Rocco looked puzzled. "Affie Hildegarde ?" He scanned the ceiling. "Who 'ees thees womans ? For why you wanna' know ?"

"It's nothing."

He was sure of it. Rocco hurried after him down the hall, shouting at him from the top of the stairs. "Hey you keed! Where you go now ?"

"Home."

"Good," Rocco said. "Home, she'sa good place for keeds."

He did not belong here. Half way up Hildegarde Road he knew he dared not confront his father. He had no right here. His presence was intrusive, impudent. How could he tell his father to come home ? Suppose his father answered : you get the hell out of here ? And that, he knew, was exactly what his father would say. He had best turn around and go home for he was moving in a sphere beyond his experience. Up there with his father was a woman. That made it different. Now he remembered something : once when he was younger he sought his father at the poolhall. His father rose from the table and followed him outside. Then he put his fingers around my throat not hard but meaning it, and he said: don't do that again.

He was afraid of his father, scared to death of his father.

In his life he had got but three beatings. Only three, but they had been violent, terrifying, unforgettable.

No thank you: never again.

He stood in the shadows of the deep pines that grew down to the circular driveway, where an expanse of lawn spread itself to the stone cottage. There was a light behind the Venetian blinds in the two front windows, but the blinds served their purpose. The sight of that cottage, so clear in moonlight and the glare of the white mountains towering in the west, such a beautiful place, made him very proud of his father. No use talking: this was pretty swell. His father was a lowdown dog and all those things, but he was in that cottage now, and it certainly proved something. You couldn't be very lowdown if you could move in on something like that. You're quite a guy, Papa. You're killing. Mamma, but you're wonderful. You and me both. Because someday I'll be doing it too, and her name is Rosa Pinelli.

He tiptoed across the gravel driveway to a strip of soggy lawn moving in the direction of the garage and the garden behind the house. A disarray of cut stone, planks, mortar boxes, and a sand screen in the garden told him that his father was working here. On tiptoe, he made his way to the place. The thing he was building, whatever it was, stood out like a black mound, straw and canvas covering it to prevent the mortar from freezing.

Suddenly he was bitterly disappointed. Perhaps his father

wasn't living here at all. Maybe he was just a common
ordinary bricklayer who went away every night and came
back in the morning. He lifted the canvas. It was a stone
bench or something; he didn't care. The whole thing was
a hoax. His father wasn't living with the richest woman
in town. Hell, he was only working for her. In disgust he
walked back to the road, down the middle of the gravel
path, too disillusioned to bother about the crunch and squeal
of gravel under his feet.

As he reached the pines, he heard the click of a latch.
Immediately he was flat on his face in a bed of wet pine
needles, a bar of light from the cottage door spearing the
bright night. A man came through the door and stood on
the edge of the short porch, the red tip of a lighted cigar
like a red marble near his mouth. It was Bandini. He looked
into the sky and took deep breaths of the cold air. Arturo
shuddered with delight. Holy Jumping Judas, but he looked
swell! He wore bright red bedroom slippers, blue pajamas,
and a red lounging robe that had white tassels on the sash
ends. Holy Jumping Jiminy, he looked like Helmer the
banker and President Roosevelt. He looked like the King
of England. O boy, what a man! After his father went inside and closed the door behind him he hugged the earth
with delight, digging his teeth into acrid pine needles. To
think that he had come up here to bring his father home!
How crazy he had been. Not for anything would he ever

disturb that picture of his father in the splendor of that new world. His mother would have to suffer; he and his brothers would have to go hungry. But it was worth it. Ah, how wonderful he had looked! As he hurried down the hill, skipping, sometimes tossing a stone into the ravine, his mind fed itself voraciously upon the scene he had just left.

But one look at the wasted, sunken face of his mother sleeping the sleep that brought no rest, and he hated his father again.

He shook her.

"I saw him," he said.

She opened her eyes and wet her lips.

"Where is he?"

"He lives down in the Rocky Mountain Hotel. He's in the same room with Rocco, just him and Rocco together."

She closed her eyes and turned away from him, pulling her shoulder away from the light touch of his hand. He undressed, darkened the house, and crawled into bed, pressing himself against August's hot back until the chill of the sheets had worn away.

Sometime during the night he was aroused, and he opened his sticky eyes to find her sitting at his side, shaking him awake. He could scarcely see her face, for she had not switched on the light.

"What did he say?" she whispered.

"Who?" But he remembered quickly and sat up. "He

said he wanted to come home. He said you won't let him. He said you'll kick him out. He was afraid to come home."

She sat up proudly.

"He deserves it," she said. "He can't do that to me."

"He looked awfully blue and sad. He looked sick."

"Huh!" she said.

"He wants to come home. He feels lousy."

"It's good for him," she said, arching her back. "Maybe he'll learn what a home means after this. Let him stay away a few more days. He'll come crawling on his knees. I know that man."

He was so tired, asleep even as she spoke.

The deep days, the sad days.

When he awoke the next morning, he found August wide-eyed too, and they listened to the noise that had awakened them. It was Mamma in the front room, pushing the carpet sweeper back and forth, the carpet sweeper that went squeakedy-bump, squeakedy-bump. Breakfast was bread and coffee. While they ate she made their lunches out of what remained of yesterday's chicken. They were very pleased: she wore her nice blue housedress, and her hair was tightly combed, tighter than they had ever seen it, rolled in a coil on the top of her head. Never before had they seen her ears so plainly. Her hair was usually loose, hiding them. Pretty ears, small and pink.

August talking:

"Today's Friday. We have to eat fish."

"Shut your holy face!" Arturo said.

"I didn't know it was Friday," Federico said. "Why did you have to tell us, August."

"Because he's a holy fool," Arturo said.

"It's no sin to eat chicken on Friday, if you can't afford fish," Maria said.

Right. Hurray for Mamma. They yah-yah-yahed August, who snorted his contempt. "Just the same, I'm not going to eat chicken today."

"Okay, sucker."

But he was adamant. Maria made him a lunch of bread dipped in olive oil and sprinkled with salt. His share of the chicken went to his two brothers.

Friday. Test day. No Rosa.

Pssssst, Gertie. She popped her gum and looked his way. No, she hadn't seen Rosa.

No, she didn't know if Rosa was in town.

No, she hadn't heard anything. Even if she did, she wouldn't tell him. Because, to be very honest about it, she would rather not talk to him.

"You cow," he said. "You milk cow always chewing your cud."

"Dago!"

He purpled, half rose out of his desk.

"You dirty little blonde bitch!"

She gasped, buried her face in horror.

Test day. By ten thirty he knew he had flunked Geometry. At the noon bell he was still fighting the English Composition quiz. He was the last person in the room, he and Gertie Williams. Anything to get through before Gertie. He ignored the last three questions, scooped up his papers, and turned them in. At the cloak-room door, he looked over his shoulder and sneered triumphantly at Gertie, her blonde hair awry, her small teeth feverishly gnawing the end of her pencil. She returned his glance with one of unspeakable hatred, with eyes that said, I'll get you for this, Arturo Bandini: I'll get you.

At two o'clock that afternoon she had her revenge.

Psssssst, Arturo.

The note she had written fell on his history book. That glittering smile on Gertie's face, the wild look in her eyes, and her jaws that had stopped moving, told him not to read the note. But he was curious.

Dear Arturo Bandini:

Some people are too smart for their own good, and some people are just plain foreigners who can't help it. You may think you are very clever, but a lot of people in this school hate you, Arturo Bandini. But the person who hates you most is Rosa Pinelli. She hates you more than

I do, because I know you are a poor Italian boy and if you look dirty all the time I do not care. I happen to know that some people who haven't got anything will steal, so I was not surprised when someone (guess who?) told me you stole jewelry and gave it to her daughter. But she was too honest to keep it, and I think she showed character in giving it back. Please don't ask me about Rosa Pinelli anymore, Arturo Bandini, because she can't stand you. Last night Rosa told me you made her shiver because you were so terrible. You are a foreigner, so maybe that's the reason. GUESS WHO????

He felt his stomach floating away from him, and a sickly smile played with his trembling lips. He turned slowly and looked at Gertie, his face stupid and smiling sickly. In her pale eyes was an expression of delight and regret and horror. He crushed the note, slumped down as far as his legs would reach, and hid his face. Save for the roar of his heart, he was dead, neither hearing, seeing, nor feeling.

In a little while he was conscious of a whispered hubbub about him, of a restlessness and excitement flitting through the room. Something had happened, the air fluttered with it. Sister Superior turned away and Sister Celia came back to her desk on the rostrum.

"The class will rise and kneel."

They arose, and in the hush no one looked away from

the nun's calm eyes. "We have just received tragic news from the university hospital," she said. "We must be brave, and we must pray. Our beloved classmate, our beloved Rosa Pinelli, died of pneumonia at two o'clock this afternoon."

There was fish for dinner because Grandma Donna had sent five dollars in the mail. A late dinner: it was not until eight o'clock that they sat down. Nor was there any reason for it. The fish was baked and finished long before that, but Maria kept it in the oven. When they gathered at the table there was some confusion, August and Federico fighting for places. Then they saw what it was. Mamma had set up Papa's place again.

"Is he coming?" August said.

"Of course he's coming," Maria said. "Where else would your father eat?"

Queer talk. August studied her. She was wearing another clean housedress, this time the green one, and she ate a lot. Federico gobbled his milk and wiped his mouth.

"Hey Arturo. Your girl died. We had to pray for her."

He was not eating, dabbing the fish in his plate with the end of his fork. For two years he had bragged to his parents and brothers that Rosa was his girl. Now he had to eat his words.

"She wasn't my girl. She was just a friend."

But he bowed his head, averting the gaze of his mother,

· 243 ·

her sympathy coming across the table to him, suffocating him.

"Rosa Pinelli, dead?" she asked. "When?"

And while his brothers supplied the answers the crush and warmth of her sympathy poured upon him, and he was afraid to raise his eyes. He pushed back his chair and arose.

"I'm not very hungry."

He kept his eyes away from her as he entered the kitchen and passed through to the back yard. He wanted to be alone so he could let go and release the constriction in his chest, because she hated me and I made her shiver, but his mother wouldn't let him, she was coming from the dining room, he could hear her footsteps, and he got up and hurried through the back yard and down the alley.

"Arturo!"

He walked down the pasture where his dogs were buried, where it was dark and he couldn't be seen, and then he cried and panted, sitting with his back against the black willow, because she hated me, because I was a thief, but Oh hell Rosa, I stole it from my mother and that isn't really stealing, but a Christmas present, and I cleared it up too, I went to confessional and got it all cleared up.

From the alley he heard his mother calling him, calling out to tell her where he was. "I'm coming," he answered, making sure his eyes were dry, licking the taste of tears from his lips. He climbed the barbed wire fence at the corner of the pasture, and she came toward him in the middle of the alley, wearing a shawl and peering secretively over her shoulder in the direction of the house. Quickly she pried open his tight fist.

"Shhhhhhh. Don't say a word to August or Federico."

He opened his palm and found a fifty cent piece.

"Go to the show," she whispered. "Buy yourself some ice-cream with the rest. Shhhhhhh. Not a word to your brothers."

He turned away indifferently, walking down the alley, the coin meaningless in his fist. She called him after a few yards, and he returned.

"Shhhhhhh. Not a word to your father. Try to get home before he does."

He walked down to the drug store across from the filling station and sucked up a milk shake without tasting it. A crowd of collegians came in and took up all seats at the soda-fountain. A tall girl in her early twenties sat beside him. She loosened her scarf and threw back the collar of her leather jacket. He watched her in the mirror behind the soda-fountain, the pink cheeks flushed and alive from the cold night air, the grey eyes huge and spilling excitement. She saw him staring at her through the glass and she turned and gave him a smile, her teeth even and sparkling.

"Hello there!" she said, her smile the sort reserved for younger boys. He answered, "Hi," and she said nothing more to him and became absorbed in the collegian on the other side of her, a grim fellow wearing a silver and gold "C" on his chest. The girl had a vigor and radiance that made him forget his grief. Over the etherial odor of drugs and patent medicines he scented the fragrance of lilac perfume. He watched the long, tapering hands and the fresh thickness of her strong lips as she sipped her coke, her pinkish throat pulsing as the liquid went down. He paid for his drink and lifted himself off the fountain stool. The girl turned to see him go, that thrilling smile her way of saying goodbye. No more than that, but when he stood outside the drugstore he was convinced that Rosa Pinelli was not dead, that it had been a false report, that she was alive and breathing and laughing like the college girl in the store, like all the girls in the world.

Five minutes later, standing under the street lamp in front of Rosa's darkened house, he gazed in horror and misery at the white and ghastly thing gleaming in the night, the long silk ribbons swaying as a gust of wind caressed them: the mark of the dead, a funeral wreath. Suddenly his mouth was full of dust-like spittle. He turned and walked down the street. The trees, the sighing trees! He quickened his pace. The wind, the cold and lonely wind! He began to run. The dead, the awful dead! They were upon him, thundering upon him out of the night sky, calling him and moaning to him, tumbling and rolling to seize him. Like mad he ran,

the streets shrieking with the echo of his pattering feet, a
cold and haunting clamminess in the middle of his back.
He took the short-cut over the trestle bridge. He fell, stumbling over a railroad tie, sprawling hands first into the cold,
freezing embankment. He was running again even before
he crawled to his feet, and he stumbled and went down
and rose up again and rushed away. When he reached his
own street, he trotted, and when he was only a few yards
from his own home, he slowed down to an easy walk,
brushing the dirt from his clothes.

Home.

There it was, a light in the front window. Home, where
nothing ever happened, where it was warm and where there
was no death.

"Arturo . . . ."

His mother was standing in the door. He walked past
her and into the warm front room, smelling it, feeling it,
revelling in it. August and Federico were already in bed. He
undressed quickly, frantically, in the semi-darkness. Then
the light from the front room went out and the house was
dark.

"Arturo?"

He walked to her bedside.

"Yes?"

She threw back the covers and tugged at his arm.

"In here, Arturo. With me."

His very fingers seemed to burst into tears as he slipped beside her and lost himself in the soothing warmth of her arms.

The rosary for Rosa.

He was there that Sunday afternoon, kneeling with his classmates at the Blessed Virgin's Altar. Far down in front, their dark heads raised to the waxon madonna, were Rosa's parents. They were such big people, there was so much of them to be shaken and convulsed as the priest's dry intonation floated through the cold church like a tired bird doomed to lift its wings once more on a journey that had no end. This was what happened when you died: Some day he would be dead and somewhere on the earth this would happen again. He would not be there but it was not necessary to be there, for this would already be a memory. He would be dead, and yet the living would not be unknown to him, for this would happen again, a memory out of life before it had been lived.

Rosa, my Rosa, I cannot believe that you hated me, for there is no hate where you are now, here among us and yet far away. I am only a boy Rosa, and the mystery of where you are is no mystery when I think of the beauty of your face and the laughter of your galoshes when you walked down the hall. Because you were such a honey, Rosa, you were such a good girl, and I wanted you, and a fellow can't be so bad if he loves a girl so good as you. And if you hate me now, Rosa, and I cannot believe that you hate me now, then look upon my grief and believe that I want you here, for that is good too. I know that you cannot come back, Rosa my true love, but there is in this cold church this afternoon a dream of your presence, a comfort in your forgiveness, a sadness that I cannot touch you, because I love you and I will love you forever, and when they gather on some tomorrow for me, then I shall have known it even before they gather, and it will not be strange to us . . .

After the services they gathered for a moment in the vestibule. Sister Celia, sniffling into a tiny handkerchief, called for quiet. Her glass eye, they noticed, had rolled around considerably, the pupil barely visible.

"The funeral will be at nine tomorrow," she said. "The eighth grade class will be dismissed for the day."

"Hot dog—what a break!"

The nun speared him with her glass eye. It was Gonzalez, the class moron. He backed to the wall and pulled his neck far into his shoulders, grinning his embarrassment.

"You!" the nun said. "It *would* be you!"

He grinned helplessly.

"The eighth grade boys will please gather in the classroom immediately after we leave the Church. The girls are excused."

They crossed the churchyard in silence, Rodriguez, Morgan, Kilroy, Heilman, Bandini, O'Brien, O'Leary, Harrington, and all the others. No one spoke as they climbed the stairs and walked to their desks on the first floor. Mutely they stared at Rosa's dust-covered desk, her books still in the shelf. Then Sister Celia entered.

"Rosa's parents have asked that you boys of her class act as pall-bearers tomorrow. Those who wish to do so will please raise their hands."

Seven hands reached for the ceiling. The nun considered them all, calling them by name to step forward. Harrington, Kilroy, O'Brien, O'Leary. Bandini. Arturo stood among those chosen, next to Harrington and Kilroy. She pondered the case of Arturo Bandini.

"No Arturo," she said. "I'm afraid you're not strong enough."

"But I am!" he insisted, glaring at Kilroy, at O'Brien at Heilman. Strong enough! They were a head taller than himself, but at one time or another he had licked them all. Nay, he could lick any two of them, at any time, day or night.

"No Arturo. Please be seated. Morgan, please step up."

He sat down, sneering at the irony of it. Ah, Rosa! He could have carried her in his arms for a thousand miles, in his own two arms to a hundred graves and back again, and yet in the eyes of Sister Celia he was not strong enough.

These nuns! They were so sweet and so gentle—and so stupid. They were all like Sister Celia: they saw from one good eye, and the other was blind and worthless. In that hour he knew that he should hate no one, but he couldn't help it: he hated Sister Celia.

Cynical and disgusted, he walked down the front steps and into the Wintry afternoon that was growing cold. Head down and hands shoved in his pockets, he started for home. When he reached the corner and looked up he saw Gertie Williams across the street, her thin shoulder blades moving under her red woolen coat. She moved slowly, her hands in the pockets of her coat that outlined her thin hips. He gritted his teeth as he thought again of Gertie's note. Rosa hates you and you make her shiver. Then Gertie heard his footstep as he mounted the curbing. She saw him and began walking fast. He had no desire to speak to her or to follow her, but the moment she quickened her steps the impulse to pursue her took him, and he was walking fast too. Suddenly, somewhere in the middle of Gertie's thin shoulder blades, he saw the truth. Rosa *hadn't* said that. Rosa *wouldn't* say that. Not about anyone. It was a lie. Gertie had written that she saw Rosa 'yesterday.' But that was impossible because on that yesterday Rosa was very sick and had died in the hospital the next afternoon.

He broke into a run and so did Gertie, but she was no match for his quickness. When he caught up with her, standing in front of her and spreading his arms to prevent her from passing, she stood in the middle of the sidewalk, her hands on her hips, defiance in her pale eyes.

"If you dare lay a hand on me, Arturo Bandini, I'll scream."

"Gertie," he said. "If you don't tell me the truth about that note I'm going to smack you right in the jaw."

"Oh, that!" she said haughtily. "A lot you know about *that!*"

"Gertie," he said "Rosa never said she hated me, and you know it."

Gertie brushed past his arm, tossed her blonde curls into the air, and said, "Well, even if she *didn't* say it, I have an idea she *thought* it."

He stood there and watched her primping down the street, throwing her head like a Shetland pony. Then he started to laugh.

10.

THE FUNERAL ON MONDAY MORNING WAS
an epilogue. He had no desire to attend; he had had
enough of sadness. After August and Federico left for
school, he sat on the steps of the front porch and opened
his chest to the warm January sun. A little while and it
would be Spring: Two or three weeks more and the big
league clubs would head south for Spring training. He
pulled off his shirt and lay face down on the dry brown
lawn. Nothing like a good tan, nothing like having one
before any other kid in town.

Pretty day, a day like a girl. He rolled to his back and
watched the clouds tumble toward the south. Up there
was the big wind; he had heard that it came all the way
from Alaska, from Russia, but the high mountains protected the town. He thought of Rosa's books, how they were
bound in blue oilcloth the color of that morning sky. Easy

day, a couple of dogs wandering by, making quick stops at every tree. He pressed his ear to the earth. Over on the North side of town, in Highland Cemetery they were lowering Rosa into a grave. He blew gently into the ground, kissed it, tasted it with the end of his tongue. Some day he would get his father to cut a stone for Rosa's grave.

The mailman stepped off the Gleason porch across the street and approached the Bandini house. Arturo arose and took the letter he offered. It was from Grandma Toscana. He brought it inside and watched his mother tear it open. There was a short message and a five-dollar bill. She pushed the five-dollar bill into her pocket and burned the message. He returned to the lawn and stretched out again.

In a little while Maria came out of the house carrying her downtown purse. He did not lift his cheek from the dry lawn, nor answer when she told him that she would return in an hour. One of the dogs crossed the lawn and sniffed his hair. He was brown and black, with huge white paws. He smiled when the big warm tongue licked his ears. He made a crook in his arm, and the dog nestled his head in it. Soon the beast was asleep. He put his ear to the furry chest and counted the heart-beat. The dog opened one eye, leaped to his feet, and licked his face with overwhelming affection. Two more dogs appeared, hurrying along, very busy along the line of trees bordering the street. The brown and black dog lifted his ears, announced himself with a cautious bark, and ran after them. They stopped and snarled, ordering him to leave them alone. Sadly the brown and black dog returned to Arturo. His heart went out to the animal.

"You stay here with me," he said. "You're my dog. You're name's Jumbo. Good old Jumbo."

Jumbo romped joyfully and attacked his face again.

He was giving Jumbo a bath in the kitchen sink when Maria returned from downtown. She shrieked, dropped her packages, and fled into the bedroom, barring the door behind her.

"Take him away!" she screamed. "Get him out of here."

Jumbo shook himself loose and rushed panic-stricken out of the house, sprinkling water and soap suds everywhere. Arturo pursued him, pleading with him to come back. Jumbo made running dives at the earth, whizzing in a wide circle, rolling on his back, and shaking himself dry. He finally disappeared into the coal shed. A cloud of coal dust rolled from the door. Arturo stood on the back porch and groaned. His mother's shrieks from the bedroom still pierced the house. He hurried to the door and quieted her, but she refused to come out until he had locked both front and back doors.

"It's only Jumbo" he soothed. "It's only my dog, Jumbo."

She went back to the kitchen and peeked through the window. Jumbo, black with coal dust, was still rushing wildly in a circle, throwing himself on his back and rushing off to do it again.

"He looks like a wolf," she said.

"He's half-wolf, but he's friendly."

"I won't have him around here," she said.

That, he knew, was the beginning of a controversy lasting for at least two weeks. It was so with all his dogs. In the end Jumbo, like his predecessors, would follow her around devotedly, with no regard for anyone else in the family.

He watched her unwrap her purchases.

Spaghetti, tomato sauce, Roman cheese. But they never had spaghetti on week-days. It was exclusively for Sunday dinner.

"How come?"

"It's a little surprise for your father."

"Is he coming home?"

"He'll be home today."

"How do you know? Did you see him?"

"Don't ask me. I just know he'll be home today."

He cut a piece of cheese for Jumbo and went out and called him. Jumbo, he discovered, could sit up. He was delighted: here was an intelligent dog, and not a mere hound dog. No doubt it was part of his wolf heritage. With Jumbo running along, his nose to the ground, sniffing and marking every tree on both sides of the street, now a block ahead of him, now a half behind him, now rushing up and barking at him, he walked Westward toward the low foothills, the white peaks towering beyond.

At the city limits, where Hildegarde Road turned sharply to the South, Jumbo growled like a wolf, surveyed the pines and underbrush on both sides of him, and disappeared into the ravine, his menacing growl a warning to whatever wild creatures that might confront him. A bloodhound! Arturo watched him weave into the brush, his belly close to the earth. What a dog! Part wolf, and part bloodhound.

A hundred yards from the crest of the hill, he heard a sound that was warm and familiar from the earliest memories of his childhood: the plinking of his father's stone mallet when it struck the dressing chisel and split the stone asunder. He was glad: it meant that his father would be in work clothes, and he liked his father in work clothes, he was easy to approach when in work clothes.

There was a crashing of thickets at his left and Jumbo rushed back to the road. Between his teeth was a dead rabbit, dead many weeks, reeking the stench of decomposition. Jumbo loped up the road a dozen yards, dropped his prey, and settled down to watching it, his chin flat on the ground, his hind quarters in the air, his eyes shifting from the rabbit to Arturo and back again. There was a savage rumble in his throat as Arturo approached . . . The stench was revolting. He rushed up and tried to kick the rabbit off the road, but Jumbo snatched it up before his foot, found the mark, and the dog dashed away, galloping triumphantly. Despite the stench Arturo watched him in admiration. Man, what a dog! Part wolf, part bloodhound, and part retriever.

But he forgot Jumbo, forgot everything, even forgot what he had planned to say as the top of his head rose above the hill and he saw his father watching him approach, the hammer in one hand, the chisel in the other. He stood on the crest of the hill and waited motionless. For a long minute Bandini stared straight into his face. Then he raised his hammer, poised the chisel, and struck the stone again. Arturo knew then that he was not unwelcome. He crossed the gravel path to the heavy bench over which Bandini worked. He had to wait a long time, blinking his eyes to avoid the flying stone chips, before his father spoke.

"Why ain't you in school?"

"No school. They had a funeral."

"Who died?"

"Rosa Pinelli."

"Mike Pinelli's girl?"

"Yes."

"He's no good, that Mike Pinelli. He scabs in the coal-mine. He's a good-for-nothing."

He went on working. He was dressing the stone, shaping it to lay along the seat of a stone-bench near the place where he worked. His face still showed the marks of Christmas

Eve, three long scratches traveling down his cheek like the marks of a brown pencil.

"How's Federico? he asked.

"He's okay."

"How's August?"

"He's all right."

Silence but for the plink of the hammer.

"How's Federico getting along in school?"

"Okay, I guess."

"What about August?"

"He's doing all right."

"What about you, You getting good marks?"

"They're okay."

Silence.

"Is Federico a good boy?"

"Sure."

"And August?"

"He's all right."

"And you?"

"I guess so."

Silence. To the north he could see the clouds gathering, the mistiness creeping upon the high peaks. He looked about for Jumbo but found no sign of him.

"Everything all right at home?"

"Everything's swell."

"Nobody sick?"

"No. We're all fine."

"Federico sleep all right at night?"

"Sure. Every night."

"And August?"

"Yep."

"And you?"

"Sure."

Finally he said it. He had to turn his back to do it, turn his back, pick up a heavy stone that called for all the strength in his neck and back and arms, so that it came with a quick gasp.

"How's Mamma?"

"She wants you to come home," he said. "She's got spaghetti cooking. She wants you at home. She told me."

He picked up another stone, larger this time, a mighty effort, his face purpling. Then he stood over it, breathing hard. His hand went to his eye, the finger brushing away a trickle at the side of his nose.

"Something in my eye," he said. "A little piece of stone."

"I know. I've had them."

"How's Mamma?"

"All right. Swell."

"She's not mad anymore?"

"Naw. She wants you home. She told me. Spaghetti for dinner. That isn't being mad."

"I don't want no more trouble," Bandini said.

"She don't even know you're here. She thinks you live with Rocco Saccone."

Bandini searched his face.

"But I *do* live with Rocco," he said. "I been there all the time, ever since she kicked me out."

A cold-blooded lie.

"I know it," he said. "I told her."

"You told her," Bandini put down his hammer "How do you know?"

"Rocco told me."

Suspiciously: "I see."

"Papa, when you coming home?"

He whistled absently, some tune without a melody, just a whistle without meaning. "I may never come home," he said. "How do you like that?"

"Mamma wants you. She expects you. She misses you."

He hitched up his belt.

"So she misses me! And what of that?"

Arturo shrugged.

"All I know is that she wants you home."

"Maybe I'll come—and maybe I won't."

Then his face writhed, his nostrils quivering. Arturo smelled it too. Behind him squatted Jumbo, the carcass between his front paws, his big tongue dripping saliva as he looked toward Bandini and Arturo and made them know he wanted to play tag again.

"Beat it, Jumbo!" Arturo said. "Take that out of here!"

Jumbo showed his teeth, the rumble emerged from his throat, and he laid his chin over the body of the rabbit. It was a gesture of defiance. Bandini held his nose.

"Whose dog?" he twanged.

"He's mine. His name's Jumbo."

"Get him out of here."

But Jumbo refused to budge. He showed his long fangs when Arturo came near, rising on his hind legs as if ready to spring, the savage gutteral muttering in his throat sounding murderously. Arturo watched with fascination and admiration.

"You see," he said. "I can't go near him. He'll tear me to ribbons."

Jumbo must have understood. The gurgle in his throat rose to a terrifying steadiness. Then he slapped the rabbit with his paw, picked it up, and walked away serenely, his tail wagging. . . . He reached the edge of the pines when the side door opened and the Widow Hildegarde emerged, sniffing precariously.

"Good heavens, Svevo! What *is* that awful smell?"

Over his shoulder Jumbo saw her. His glance shifted to the pines and then back again. He dropped the rabbit, picked it up with a firmer grip, and strolled sensuously across the lawn toward the Widow Hildegarde. She was in no mood to caper. Seizing a broom, she walked out to meet him. Jumbo raised his lips, peeling them back until his huge white teeth glistened in the sun, strings of saliva dripping from his jaws. He released his gurgle, savage, bloodcurdling, a warning that was both a hiss and a growl. The Widow stopped in her tracks, composed herself, studied the dog's mouth, and tossed her head in annoyance. Jumbo dropped his burden and unrolled his long tongue in satisfaction. He had mastered them all. Closing his eyes, he pretended to be asleep.

"Get that goddam dog outa' here!" Bandini said.

"Is that your dog?" the Widow asked.

Arturo nodded with subdued pride.

The Widow searched his face, then Bandini's.

"Who is this young man?" she asked.

"He's my oldest boy," Bandini said.

The Widow said: "Get that horrible thing off my grounds."

Ho, so she was that kind of a person! So that was the kind of a person she was! Immediately he made up his mind to do nothing about Jumbo, for he knew the dog was playing. And yet he like to believe that Jumbo was as ferocious as he pretended. He started toward the dog, walking deliberately, slowly. Bandini stopped him.

"Wait," he said. "Let me handle this."

He seized the hammer and studied his pace toward Jumbo, who wagged his tail and vibrated as he panted.

Bandini was within ten feet of him before he rose to his hind legs, stretched out his chin, and commenced his warning growl. That look on his father's face, that determination to kill which rose out of bravado and pride because the Widow was standing there, sent him across the grass and with both arms he seized the short hammer and knocked it from Bandini's tight fist. At once Jumbo sprang to action, leaving his prey and prowling steadily toward Bandini, who backed away. Arturo dropped to his knees and held Jumbo. The dog licked his face, growled at Bandini, and licked his face again. Every movement of Bandini's arm brought an answering snarl from the dog. Jumbo wasn't playing anymore. He was ready to fight.

"Young man," the Widow said. "Are you going to take that dog out of here, or shall I call the police and have him shot?"

It infuriated him.

"Don't you dare, damn you!"

Jumbo leered at the Widow and showed his teeth.

"Arturo!" Bandini remonstrated. "That's no way to talk to Mrs. Hildegarde."

Jumbo turned to Bandini and silenced him with a snarl.

"You contemptible little monster" the Widow said. "Svevo Bandini, are you going to allow this vicious boy to carry on like this?"

"Arturo!" Bandini snapped.

"You peasants!" the Widow said. "You foreigners! You're all alike, you and your dogs and all of you."

Svevo crossed the lawn toward the Widow Hildegarde. His lips parted. His hands were folded before him.

Mrs. Hildegarde," he said. "That's my boy. You can't talk to him like that. That boy's an American. He is no foreigner."

"I'm talking to you too!" The Widow said.

"Bruta animale!" he said. *"Puttana!"*

He spattered her face with spittle.

"Animal that your are!" he said *"Animal!"*

He turned to Arturo.

"Come on," he said. "Let's go home."

The Widow stood motionless. Even Jumbo sensed her fury and slunk away, leaving his noisome booty before her on the lawn. At the gravel path where the pines opened to the road down the hill, Bandini stopped to look back. His face was purple. He raised his fist.

"Animal!" he said.

Arturo waited a few yards down the road. Together they descended the hard reddish trail. They said nothing, Bandini still panting from rage. Somewhere in the ravine Jumbo roamed, the thicket crackling as he plunged through. The clouds had banked at the peaks, and though the sun still shone, there was a touch of cold in the air.

"What about your tools?" Arturo said.

"They're not my tools. They're Rocco's. Let him finish the job. That's what he wanted anyway."

Out of the thicket rushed Jumbo. He held a dead bird in his mouth, a very dead bird, dead many days now.

"That damn dog!" Bandini said.

"He's a good dog, Papa. He's part bird dog."

Bandini looked at a patch of blue in the East.

"Pretty soon we'll have Spring," he said.

"We sure will!"

Even as he spoke something tiny and cold touched the back of his hand. He saw it melt, a small star-shaped snowflake. . . .

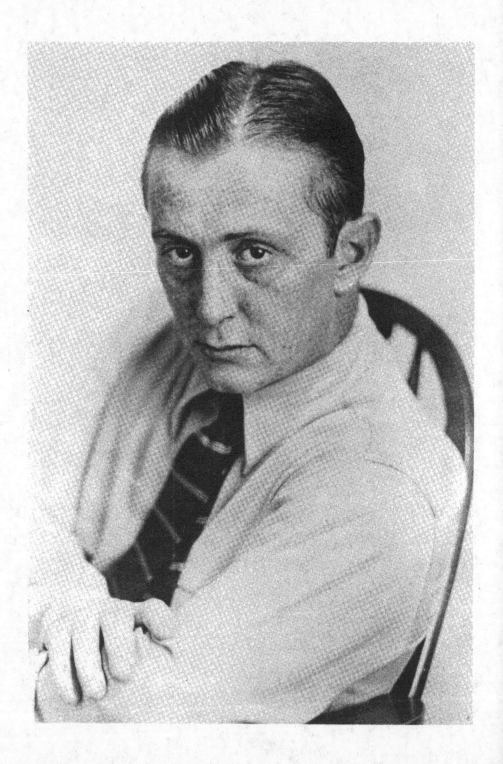

JOHN FANTE was born in Colorado in 1909. He attended parochial school in Boulder, and Regis High School, a Jesuit boarding school. He also attended the University of Colorado and Long Beach City College.

Fante began writing in 1929 and published his first short story in *The American Mercury* in 1932. He published numerous stories in *The Atlantic Monthly*, *The American Mercury*, *The Saturday Evening Post*, *Collier's*, *Esquire*, and *Harper's Bazaar*. His first novel, *Wait Until Spring, Bandini* was published in 1938. The following year *Ask the Dust* appeared, and in 1940 a collection of his short stories, *Dago Red*, was published and is now collected in *The Wine of Youth*.

Meanwhile, Fante had been occupied extensively in screenwriting. Some of his credits include *Full of Life*, *Jeanne Eagels*, *My Man and I*, *The Reluctant Saint*, *Something for a Lonely Man*, *My Six Loves* and *Walk on the Wild Side*.

John Fante was stricken with diabetes in 1955 and its complications brought about his blindness in 1978, but he continued to write by dictation to his wife, Joyce, and the result was *Dreams from Bunker Hill* (1982). He died at the age of 74 on May 8, 1983.